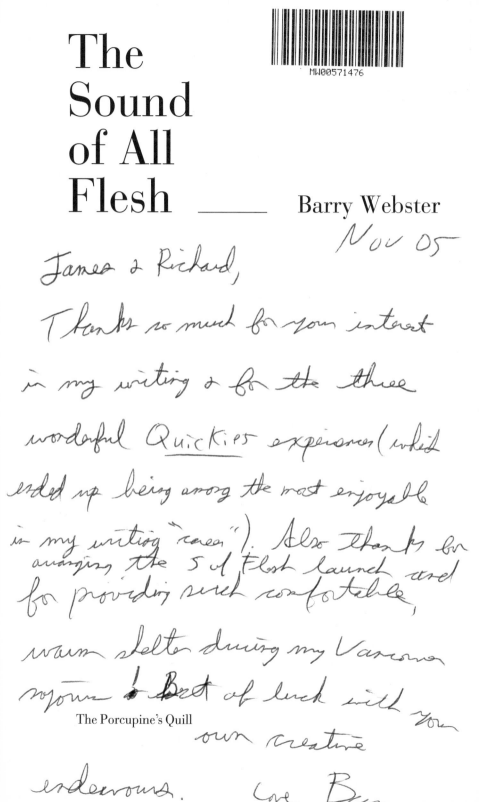

The Sound of All Flesh

Barry Webster

Nov 05

James & Richard,

Thanks so much for your interest in my writing & for the three wonderful Quickies experiences (which ended up being among the most enjoyable in my writing "career"). Also thanks for arranging the S of Flesh launch and for providing such comfortable, warm shelter during my Vancouver sojourn & Best of luck with your own creative endeavours. Love Bar

The Porcupine's Quill

Library and Archives Canada Cataloguing in Publication

Webster, Barry, date
The sound of all flesh/by Barry Webster.

Short stories.
ISBN-13: 978-0-88984-280-9.--
ISBN-10: 0-88984-280-9

I. Title.

PS8595.E343S68 2005   c813'.6   C2005-904545-0

Published by The Porcupine's Quill,
68 Main Street, Erin, Ontario NOB 1TO.
www.sentex.net/~pql

Readied for the press by Jack Illingworth; copy edited by Doris Cowan.

Represented in Canada by the Literary Press Group.
Trade orders are available from University of Toronto Press.

We acknowledge the support of the Ontario Arts Council,
and the Canada Council for the Arts for our publishing program.
The financial support of the Government of Canada
through the Book Publishing Industry Development Program
and the BPIDP Internship Program is also gratefully acknowledged.
Thanks, also, to the Government of Ontario through the Ontario
Media Development Corporation's Ontario Book Initiative.

Canada Council
for the Arts
Conseil des Arts
du Canada

ONTARIO ARTS COUNCIL
CONSEIL DES ARTS DE L'ONTARIO

The Sound of All Flesh

For Robert Jennings

Table of Contents

'To listen is an effort, and just to hear is no merit. A duck hears also.'
– Igor Stravinsky

The Royal Conservatory
Statement and Fugue for Eight Voices

ALLEGRO (♪ = 108)   OP. 64, No. 2

Statement

MEZZO-PIANO

1: The Royal Conservatory of Music looms like a castle, a battleship, a mortuary, a cathedral. Its rooms are like matchboxes, amphitheatres, half-lit caves, telephone booths. There one smells fumes of daffodils, drying resin, tour buses, lemon wax. Outside it zoom BMWs, paper airplanes, high-frequency radio waves, humming-birds.

The Royal Conservatory of Music blooms like a chrysanthemum, a dandelion, a cheese soufflé, the ember in the end of a lit cigarette.

2: Sitting in my over-upholstered office and gazing out through the latticed windows at the frost-covered courtyard, the empty, circular, cement fountain, dangling icicles, dead squirrels, and trees reft by lightning, I think it has been a good life I've lived here as a piano teacher at the Royal Conservatory of Music, and as I hear the metronome-like click-click-click of the accordion-shaped radiator, it's as if my name's being repeated Ted-Ted-Ted-Sims piano teacher extraordinaire, oh not extraordinaire but OK, fine, accomplished and content, and as I stand, open the door and place my gold-buckled shoe on the speckled, tiled floor and head out into the half-lit corridor where the glorious sound of the tremulous glissandos of contrabasses mixes with the booming roar of pianos played in the lower register with the pedal down, accentuated by the sudden, bright, staccato squawk of people whose throats are being slit, the sound rises and falls and one feels one's submerged in tossing ocean waves or is being beaten on the forehead with a blunt machete, and

II

as I step between corridor walls covered with paintings of my old, beloved colleagues, past the balustrades adorned with vases of tulips, baskets full of hissing scorpions or the severed, still-beating hearts of romantic composers from the mid-nineteenth century whose blood drips in straight lines down the wallpaper and coagulates in little puddles just below the electric sockets, I think with pleasure of the joy, the wonder, the cracked jaws and kicked scrotums inherent in every bar of every piece I've ever taught, and as I approach the main lobby, I remember the conservatory's star students, now professional musicians, the harpist who won first prize in the Vienna Mozart festival, the flautist who stabbed her instrument into her boyfriend's stomach cavity, the two mezzo-sopranos who gouged out each others' eyes with ice picks and I think the Conservatory is a magnificent place and I have lived a magnificent life and how hard it will be for me to retire and renounce my magic powers and become like mortal men, and as I, for the last time ever, push open the Royal Conservatory of Music's heavy, lacquered, oak door that I've stepped through a million times before, and look out at the street, which I realize is no longer a street but a fire-filled abyss within which writhe shrieking, blood-spattered, goblin-faced figures, and flailing, still-alive, half-dismembered corpses, their intestines dangling like tangled treble clefs, then, making sure my tie is straight, I take one step and fall forward.

3: Miss Rumpelstiltit plays the piano in a style oh-so-elegant. Elegant. Swelligant. Intelligent. She is magnificent. Look, as her wrist superbly arches as she delicately, oh so delicately plays the couplets in Mozart's Sonata in A Major. And oh her pianissimo is so delicate, swellicate, immellicate. Hear the phrases soft as fingers pressed against the downy breasts of birds that don't squawk but warble, pharble, tarble. Oh Miss Rumpelstiltit, play on, play on. And she does. Mozart's cadenza not influenza nor cumenza but slupenza, nermenza and even chorpenza. And now listen as her hand lifts and there is a pause, a silence, a mysterious void where the deafening racket of our ever-babbling lives stops and the whole universe leans forward with its ear cocked listening for that secret concealed in a double quarter rest. There it is. Do you hear it? Then Miss Rumpelstiltit's hand slowly descends and plays five clear, bell-like notes, like a diagonal line stretching across a blank canvas, and life returns, wraps round me in a warm embrace as – elegant, swelligent, immelligent, the main theme returns like a lost dove flying home to snuggle, nestle in my arms, cooing, joyful, ecstatic – relligent, velligent, onselligent!

4: In the Conservatory basement whenever the students run their bows across their violins, the horsehair cuts through the strings, then saws into the instrument's wood frame, severing the top half, which falls to the ground with a loud thud. The cellos have been splitting in half sideways, and when the viola players place their instruments under their necks, the lacquered bodies disintegrate into hundreds of unjoinable pieces that make a terrible clattering sound as they strike the floor and get stuck in people's shoes when they're accidentally stepped on. The Royal Conservatory's head office has been getting complaints from both students and parents and the janitor is growing tired of sweeping up the sawdust.

But just this week it got worse. One thought only the string section was affected, but at Monday's rehearsal when the harpist touched her instrument, all the wires snapped at once, then the percussionist struck the snare drum which exploded like a balloon pricked with a needle, and the knob on his drumstick flew off and began bouncing about the room like a ping-pong ball. Now the trumpets' horns repeatedly fall off and roll back and forth across the floor, sometimes hitting people's ankles, and when the trombonists thrust forward their slides, they dislodge and shoot straight across the room, breaking windows or getting stuck in walls, as the bassoons ascend like rockets into the ceiling. The rehearsals take place in a whirlwind of flying instrument parts and ceiling-plaster falling like rain. Then yesterday, when the tuba sounded its lowest note, it emitted a noxious gas and all the choir members fainted, the flutes went limp like sagging strings of toffee, as the clarinets dissolved to

13

mercury that made a loud hissing sound as it dribbled down the students' legs.

Unfortunately, parents had to pay for all the practices in advance and the Conservatory is sticking to its no-refunds policy.

Mrs Johnstone, Stephanie's mother, is outraged. 'I paid good money for my daughter to become musical but I didn't expect all this tumult and racket.'

Mrs Binkley said, 'I can understand a few difficulties, but this is absolutely ridiculous. I'm afraid the experience might make my Bobbie tone deaf if it doesn't turn him off music altogether.'

Ms Price told us, 'It's very dangerous for the children. The shooting trombone slides could easily hit someone in the head, and the snapping harp strings could take someone's eye out.'

The President of the Royal Conservatory of Music has assured parents that with time the students' playing will improve. In the end, however, no one is sure if it's really the students or the instruments who are not co-operating.

5: Not eating margarine would mean undermining my integrity as an artist. I know you're all thinking, well, doesn't that make you a very vain woman? But I feel vanity is a part of art and the non-vain are really non-artistic.

Each night before I sing, I rub margarine across my face and forehead; I massage some through my hair. I squeeze crescents of it into my ears. Then I bite into large cakes of it trying to get some stuck between my teeth. Margarine makes me feel free. It reminds me that I'm a woman and a human being and a magnificent performer and that most people would suck the shit from my ass if they could be me for one hour. Margarine brings me peace and teaches me the value of life.

Sometimes when I roll margarine into wax-paper-coated tubes and stick them up my nostrils, or after smearing swaths of it over my eyes, I feel truly spiritual. Last week as I fingered the Becel label, I began weeping. I swallowed a bowlful, spread some on my kneecaps, the back of my neck, and shoved a cake of it up my rectum, then I had a revelation. The revelation was 'You're beautiful and life is beautiful. Keep on living. Don't give up.'

Before my performances I lie in a large tub of margarine. I am coated in margarine as if in Holy light. Later I shower and, as the margarine flows off my skin and down the drain, I feel I've shed all impurities, any private weaknesses, humiliating moments of fear, notes accidentally sung in the lower register. I am a soprano.

In the concert hall I stand before my audience. I think: I am golden light. I am better than you all. I am margarine.

3: Oh Miss Rumpelstiltit, you are a sly one. At first elegant, swelligent, and now in the second movement, a whole new repertoire, effect, and let us say it, register. Your fingers dance as on a hot iron plate – pick-pock sick-sock rick-rock – like a bunch of toy hammers pock-picking against one's head – lock-lick mock-mick dock-dick – a group of tiny people scurrying about the deck of a ship that's sinking – sock-sick nock-nick chock-chick – or ants crawling in and out of the hair follicles of a man half-asleep on a desert island – rock-rick shock-shick fock-fick – oh Miss Rumpelstiltit you're a shrewd one, you're a feisty cracker – nock-nick thock-thick – watch her fingers like scalpels – dock-dick – chisels – sock-sick – dancing Popsicle sticks – sock-sick bock-bick, oh Miss Rum-pel-stil-tik you know your mu-sic makes me dock-dick stock-stick it's all too knock-nick notes like fingers dock-dick touching feeling pock-pick probing every orifice in my body.

6: Because I play the oboe, I should die. My ears should be torn off with pliers, my chest gashed and ribs rent from my chest one by one, my head, pelvis, and limbs shredded and devoured by the daggersharp teeth of fierce, leaping hordes of savage, famished jackals, grizzly bears, tigers and hyenas.

Oh everybody says, 'The oboe's sound is so exotic, faraway.' 'There's only one oboe in any orchestra because its sound is so particular.' Which means I'm a freak. I can't stand the sight of my face in the mirror: eyeballs like pulsating maggots, cheeks and forehead a fetid mass of exploding, volcano-cratered, pus-spewing acne, ghastly, ten-ton, rusted-iron-bar glasses held together with masking tape coated in dripping mould, cracked, bloody lips displaying rotting teeth and festering gums about which pus-headed worms writhe.

If I could roll up in a corner and put a bullet through my brain but I don't have a bullet, brain or even a corner, I live in the garbage dump just out of town where I suck out the remains from the bottom of soup-tins and swallow clods of shit-crusted earth to survive. But worst of all, once a month Federal Express arrives with a message, 'We need you to play *Rite of Spring*,' or 'We still need an oboe for the Pastoral Symphony' and I must haul myself out of the pit full of muck, piss and vomit where I lie moaning, put on a tie and appear before PEOPLE.

Now I sit beside the other wind players, whose instruments correctly have one reed, unlike my freak-horn which has two.

Eyes closed, trembling so much my knees are making the music stand rattle, I count the bars, twenty before the orchestra stops and I must play the solo in the First Movement of Beethoven's Fifth Symphony – six long, drawn-out notes, F E-flat D F E-flat D, against a backdrop of silence. Unprotected, naked, bare, exposed to the vicious, well-dressed, steel-eyed multitudes glaring down at me through gold-plated pince-nez, ready to judge and condemn me.

Oh that I had never taken a single oboe lesson in my life, that oboes never existed, that I never existed, that music never was!

4: One night the instruments tried to escape from the Royal Conservatory of Music. Who could blame them? First the flutes carefully aimed themselves, then leapt at the doorknob buttons, releasing the locks. The woodwinds hopped clanking behind; from the east wing came the brass section scraping along the marble-tiled floor as kettledrums rumbled down steep stairways. When the first-floor lock was open, the instruments fled into the unlit parking lot, sheet music blowing from the door of the Conservatory's store. But then the grand pianos tried to fit through the door. They were too wide and, in desperation, began pounding their frames against the door jambs, finally waking the security guard, who retrieved all the escaping instruments from the outside world and locked them back in the Conservatory.

The instruments still remember their brief dash to freedom. Just for a moment they were outside the Royal Conservatory of Music, in a world without sound, no one unwantedly putting their lips on their orifices or shoving cleaning pipes down their spines. On cold winter nights when the wind moans in the rafters, the instruments, locked in their felt-lined cases, begin weeping. The sound starts slowly, then rises to fill the building. It is a haunting sound no human has ever heard, in a key none of us could ever understand.

7: Ka-ching ka-ching ka-ching ka-ching …

The Royal Conservatory of Music's guest conductor is masturbating in the third-floor washroom cubicle.

Ka-ching ka-ching ka-ching ka-ching … His belt's undone and its metal catch keeps thwacking the outer square. Ka-ching ka-ching ka-ching ka-ching …

The high-pitched sound rises up and over the cubicle walls.

It is the sound of the door-knocker at the Pearly Gates. And the sound of keys that jingle from St. Stephen's robe as, arms waving, he conducts Celestial Choirs. It is also the sound of spoon clacking teacup during long-ago visits to Aunt Beatrice whom the conductor loved, and it is the sound of muffled, tintinnabulous voices of long-lost childhood friends calling from a faraway country to which he can never return. Ka-ching ka-ching ka-ching ka-ching … It is also the sound of money being counted, the earthly money his fame brings into the Conservatory. Ka-ching ka-ching ka-ching ka-ching …

In his mind are long, lacquered violin bows, the hole at the bottom of the kettledrum he's always passed but never touched, the dark S-slits in the sides of cellos that can never be seen into even when tilted toward the light, and the abrupt, in-unison leap of viola bows that sit poised on their strings the moment he raises his hand.

Ka-ching ka-ching ka-ching ka-ching ...

He has never been able to find anything equivalent to the sound of the belt buckle in any music anywhere, and he wonders why Bach, Mendelssohn, even Beethoven didn't use it, and as the tempo increases – Ka-ching ka-ching ka-ching – he has a sudden revelation about the bringing together of violin bows and the holes in kettle-drums, the merging of piccolo sticks and the gleaming horns of tubas – KA-CHING KA-CHING KA-CHING – now he will change his life, he will not conduct any longer – and as 1,785,519 sperm, each shaped like a thirty-second note, some staccato, some marcatissimo, suddenly strike the cubicle wall, he realizes – yes, he will become a composer.

4: List of items on order for Royal Conservatory of Music Store:

• Bach's *Well-Tempered Klavier* adapted for hand-and-armpit solos.
• Béla Bartók's *Lost Show Tunes*.
• Heart of Chopin removed from tomb in St. Felic Cathedral, Krakov, Poland. (On loan for Xeroxing.)
• Sheet music in braille and, conversely, sound recordings of the world's greatest paintings.
• Clara Schumann's *Why Am I the Only Goddamned Woman Composer in the Whole Bloody Nineteenth Century?*
• Handkerchief Franz Schubert used to cough up tubercular phlegm. (On loan for Xeroxing.)
• Motivational tapes: Chopin, *I Feel and Because I Feel, I Can Do It.* Bach, *God God God.*
• *A Canadian Coupling*: Murray Schafer composes for 'The Trouble with Tracy.'
• Specially priced, corporate-sponsored metronomes installed with speakers that shout HON-DA HON-DA at lower tempos, M-BANX for Allegro, and BUY-BUY-BUY for Presto.

4: And then finally, Miss Rumpelstiltit, the return, the return I'm craving, the gathering tide, rising, whirling streams of notes climbing up and up, about to burst the dam-walls that contain them, round and round and higher and higher – and then – BELLIGANT SWELLIGANT MELLIGANT – I cry out in ecstasy – VELLIGENT WELLIGENT SWELLIGENT – tears stream down my cheeks – SMELLIGENT HELLIGENT NELLIGENT E-L-E-G-A-A-A-NT! The roar of applause and I leap up, clapping, screaming, and then she rises from the piano bench, yes, Miss Rumpelstiltit, braids of hair arranged in cornices above her lily-white forehead, she meekly steps forward and – what's happened? – she's not there! She's – what? – She's fallen onto the floor of the stage! Staring forward, not believing, I finally see it: someone has had the nerve to place a banana peel on the floor exactly where Miss Rumpelstiltit will step. Some people start laughing, and then others laugh and like fire leaping from tree to tree until the entire forest is ablaze, the hall erupts with deafening, demonic, tumultuous, pulverizing laughter. 'This is an outrage,' I cry, 'AN OUTRAGE!' but already crowds of people are swarming forwards onto the stage, each carrying a metal-legged, wood-back chair that they begin, one by one, to break over the back and beautiful head of Miss Rumpelstiltit.

8: I am the President. Of the Royal Conservatory of Music. I work hard every day. I am respected very widely. I hire the new teachers. I advertise the new concerts. I call the agents of the guest artists. I rent out rooms to a marvellous faculty and I speak to donors who bring money, lots of money into our fine institution.

I'm qualified. I have an MBA. And I have a BSc. And I have an ARCT and I've studied piano, cello and flute. I have also written music. I published articles in *Musician's Quarterly*, *Musician's Monthly* and *Adult Musician*. I can add a balance sheet. I can varnish a tabletop. I've been to Guatemala. I studied carpet embroidery with the greatest teacher of our day and I can shoot a bull's-eye dead centre at a distance of five metres. I once rode a horse through a dry riverbed and I've climbed the Leaning Tower of Pisa with suction cups on my feet. I shot terrorists in the war in Bosnia and have tracked yetis in the High Himalayas after translating the Bhagavad-

Gita into Latin and Greek. I have swum from the Indian Ocean to the Pacific, and after rounding Tierra del Fuego, I jet-skied to the North Pole. I spend my free time moving Arctic air masses back and forth between Greenland and Siberia and I've recently started stitching the holes in the ozone together with threads from the wings of gossamer angels. Sometimes I am an angel myself.

When I get tired of flying back and forth between the Throne of God and the Pearly Gates and exploring the Highest Heavens full of Archangels who are always doing their nails, clacking gum between their teeth and watching *Laverne and Shirley* reruns, I descend to Hell to crack a few jokes with Satan ('Hot enough for you?'), then push through the lower stratosphere and escape into the Milky Way, where I start planets spinning the wrong direction, hide a few of Jupiter's moons when no one's looking, rearrange the rings of Saturn so the green ones are separate from the red, and play with the thermostat-dial on the back of the sun.

Then when I'm bored I go back to the Royal Conservatory of Music to do some filing and return a few e-mails.

Last week God called me on the phone and I said, 'Geez God, business is good but I miss the old days, just you and me hanging out in a distant galaxy, playing pool with stray meteorites and making stogies out of the burnt-out asteroids.'

Someday I'm gonna blow this Popsicle stand for good and join God seven eons away for few rounds of crap and some nice, cold brewskies.

Fugue

MEZZO-FORTE

7: Ka-ching ka-ching ka-ching ka-ching

4: HON-da

   HON-da

7: Ka-ching ka-ching ka-ching ka-ching

5: Margarine

(Silence)

7: Ka-ching ka-ching ka-ching ka-ching

4: HON-da

   HON-da

7: Ka-ching ka-ching ka-ching ka-ching

5: Margarine

(Silence)

4: 'And it was dangerous because the harp strings could take some-one's eye out and already students had started swallowing bits of falling plaster.'

5: And when the margarine-flashlight shines up my vaginal canal

4: escape far from the Royal Conservatory of Music

5: lighting up the very centre of my being

4: out into the parking lot and vanishing into the night

5: I know women are superior to all men and I'm superior to all women because I am coated in margarine.

3: Velligent

6: But I can't stand their steel-eyed faces

8: I set planets spinning in the wrong direction

6: boring into mine

8: make Hula Hoops from Saturn's rings

6: as I hold my oboe like a frozen turd-stick

3: Melligent, swelligent

6: if I could have a million railway ties driven into my skull, my intestines torn out and thrown beneath the pummelling wheels of a charging, ten-ton truck and the rest of my body boiled in carbolic acid.

(Silence)

2: Making sure my tie is straight, I take one step and fall forward

3: the quarter rest's a mystery, all you have to do is listen

5: With margarine under my armpits, I know God is ever with me

2: Making sure my jacket's done up, I take one step and fall forward

3: She's elegant, swelligent and in fact yelligent and velligent

2: Making sure there's no lint on my lapel, I take one step and fall forward

4: they dream of a world without sound, the sun rising and falling in silence

2: Making sure I'm not playing pocket pool, I take one step and fall forward

8: I'll talk to God like in the old days before either of us had made it big

2: I take one step and fall forward

    I fall forward

    I fall forward

4: m-banx m-banx

    m-banx m-banx

A man plays one note on his oboe, before listeners who have daggers hidden in their pockets.

    A woman coated in margarine stands erect before a mirror.

    A president gazes skyward and contemplates life on Pluto.

    A group of non-unionized instruments plot a second escape.

    I am gazing at Miss Rumpelstiltit as the chairs go tumbling over her.

    But every floor's on fire.

    Every floor's on fire.

    Every floor's on fire.

    Every floor's on fire.

    Perhaps it's always been so but nobody noticed for the cry of smoke alarms always sounded like – music.

1: The Royal Conservatory of Music looms like a funnel cloud, a tidal wave, a dropped H-bomb, a blazing hurtling planet that has finally collided with Earth.

2: I take one step and fall –

    one step and fall –

    one step and fall –

5: As margarine seeps into all the pores in my skin I know I alone am beautiful

7: He thinks of the S-slits, the subtle curve of the harp-frame

6: My mouth on the double reed, playing F, E-flat, D –

4: The instruments huddle in the emergency exit, trembling with anticipation

3: And I run through the riotous multitudes, their chairs raised like swords, towards my prone Miss Rumpelstiltit, who gazes at me weeping and imploring

2: one step

    one step

    one step

    one step

(Silence)

(Silence)

(Silence)

(Silence)

(Silence)

(Silence)

FORTISSIMO!!!!!!!!!!!!!!!!!!!!!

4: Then the piccolo leaps, lands like a dagger in the forehead of the sleeping security guard

5: And the fire touches the foot of a woman who, because of the oil in her margarine, bursts into flame

PRESTO! PRESTO! BUY-BUY-BUY-BUY!!

6: I pull my mouth from the reed, look at the shrieking crowd, ten thousand daggers fly towards me, strike my shoulder, face, neck

5: In a margarine-blaze I'm now brighter than the sun

4: The exit door bursts open and the instruments flee into the night

3: I take Miss Rumpelstiltit in my arms, press her lips against mine

8: Arms outstretched I pierce the ozone layer, see God counting poker chips beside Neptune

2: I take one step and fall forward

    forward forward

5: I'm beautiful

2: forward

4: m-banx

4: piccolo

3: I press her body against mine and will hold on to her forever.

6: And now I know my life is over, I stab the oboe through my heart.

THE SOUND OF ALL FLESH

7: And surrounded by walls of flame, I know I'll always be a composer.

5: margarine

7: ka-ching

4: m-banx

3: swelligent

8: angel wings

4: plaster

8: angel wings

4: plaster

5: MARGARINE

(Applause)

The Innocence of Water

I was confused when the lawyer said we'd sue for emotional suffering. Wasn't some suffering unavoidable? And when he said $15,000 could be divided into allotments of $1,700 for swimmers still having nightmares, $1,800 if on medication, the amount higher for those in the deep end and steadily increasing towards the pool's centre, where I'd been, it was as if a wave washed over me and again I was in a sudden darkness, watching plaster specks whirl about my body, in a silent space where nothing is measured.

The lawyer cleared his throat. 'Those having near-death experiences should receive most.'

I put my hand on the table's varnished mahogany top, an oblong rectangle shaped very much like a swimming-pool and supported by four cylindrical iron legs, each one a metre long and two centimetres in diameter. Trivial details, but I've learned banalities determine everything. For example, the streetcar had been late that day, but not late enough for me to turn around and just go home. Also, when I arrived, everybody was already in the water. What would've happened, we wondered later, if the on-deck push-ups and sit-ups had gone on longer? Would there have been mayhem, a frenzied jostling to get into the pool, or would people have run along the deck?

I'd approached our lane as Christopher was swimming up.

'Hi, Mike,' he called.

'Hey.' Fixing my goggles, I put one foot in the pool. 'It's frigging soup, today.' 'I know.' He was treading water, red-faced. 'It's a sauna. And the air's so humid you can hardly breathe.'

Humid air, the triviality that caused everything. Later, at municipal meetings and on *CityPulse News* the city architect explained. 'We estimate the humidity was 90 per cent, abnormally high due partly to the above-average water temperature that had been raised to twenty-four degrees for the senior swim that took place earlier that afternoon. The porous drywall in the ceiling, which normally absorbs some humidity, became saturated and the moisture eventually penetrated and eroded the glue-base holding the inner ceiling to the building's outer shell. Though only two years old, the ceiling was already slightly damaged. Some swimmers said that a week prior to the incident, they'd noticed discoloured spots and slight bulges in the panelling. The particular brand of drywall used was simply not appropriate for a high-humidity environment.'

When the ceiling began to fall, most of us were at the end of the deep half, waiting for instructions from the coach. Diana, his assistant, was doing paperwork on deck. We've never been able to agree on who saw it first. The ceiling creased slightly in the middle, as the northern part began to curve down over our heads. I was saying to Christopher, 'I couldn't find my bike wheel ...', heard a shout, turned, Diana jumped up, cried 'Holy shit', ran, the ceiling touched the wall clock as she dived into the pool with her clothes on. This was the action that marked before and after. As if a stopwatch had been pressed, everyone pushed from the pool edge, started swimming forward rapidly. I didn't understand what was happening but instinctively followed. Breathing to the side, I saw the entire, white-tiled ceiling tilting at a perfect 30-degree angle to the pool; a thundering bang as one end struck the deck behind; next breath it slanted 25 degrees, then 15. It first covered the deck, then the pool's deep end, the shallow part last. I was halfway across the deep end and the ceiling hung just a few feet above my back as Tony passed, arms pummelling furiously. I thought what was happening might be funny; when the ceiling struck us, it'd break into bits of Styrofoam and laughing we'd swim about floating debris, throwing pieces at each other.

The ceiling struck my back with surprising force and was like a great hand pushing me underwater. If I'd known what was to follow, I would've taken a big breath of air before going under. Suddenly, an underwater darkness, something hard above the head that blocked out the light. A loud thud somewhere – are pillars falling into the pool too? I moved my legs, scissor-kicking, lifted my arms and tried to push upwards but the object above was immovable as a wall. I felt along what I imagined was a square ceiling panel, searching for an edge, some opening, but at the end another panel seemed to be attached. Frenzied, I felt quickly along the second panel and at its end was a third, and then at the end of this panel, an edge I could reach around, but there was something hard overhead. Were there pieces stacked on top of each other? My lungs screamed for oxygen, and I imagined briefly I was at the pool bottom with a million layers of solid debris above me. I then felt along to a fourth panel, a fifth, a sixth, water and plaster-flecks filling my goggles, my forehead being cut on ceiling nails, and at the seventh panel, I started inhaling water.

'The ceiling blocks were held together with plaster-coated strips,' the architect said, 'which unfortunately held together too well. The fallen ceiling blanketed the entire pool except for the top eighth of the shallow end. The only opening left was a narrow space around the pool's inside edge where the ceiling on deck broke from the water-bound section, plus a few small holes in the centre where light fixtures had been. Luckily the lane-ropes stretched but didn't snap, preventing the ceiling from sinking to the pool bottom.'

Days later I found myself wandering the streets of my city, gazing up at office buildings, the brutal straight lines of their walls and roofs, rows of identical square windows placed equidistant to each other, floors a series of stacked parallel lines. If one collapsed onto another, it'd fall onto the next and so on. If you remove just one small piece of a wall, the whole high-rise topples sideways; I imagined desks falling through the air, filing cabinets, steel beams, ten-storey pipes hurtling into the pavement amidst a soft splatter of bodies and rising spray of shattered glass. Pushing a cart down the supermarket aisle, I noticed the ceiling measured about twenty times larger than the short walls. In the Eaton Centre, I watched thousands of people on stairways, bridges, moving in and out of labyrinthine tunnels, and thought, it's an act of faith that allows people to get through the day safely.

In my apartment, I heard footsteps on the ceiling and wondered where my upstairs neighbour would land if he fell into my living room. My hardwood floor shines; if it collapsed and my body hit a sofa in the flat below, would I be badly hurt? If I landed on a TV, what then? Where's the best place to land?

I went to the library and read that walls and ceilings joined at perfect ninety-degree angles are more secure than those at eighty-nine or ninety-one degrees. Later, my roommate entered, saw me on a ladder and said, 'What're you doing?'

In the subway, metre-thick tunnel walls hold back tons of inpushing earth. On board, I practised holding my breath between stations. I could go one stop with no trouble; two was harder; I tried to go three, not letting myself breathe until the doors opened, then emerged gasping on the subway platform.

I went into Union Station where the ceiling is the highest of any in the city, a grey stone arch. Touching the scabs on my forehead, I thought if it had been this ceiling, the grittiness would have left linear scratches rather than dots.

The metal escalator steps banged beneath my climbing feet as I entered my bank's stone-walled lobby. I live in a world of hard substances. In the bathtub I squeezed a facecloth of water over my soft, scratched arms.

Drinking I wondered what determines whether liquid's routed to the stomach or lungs. In the throat there's a lever, turnstile, perhaps a gate flapping. I should concentrate while swallowing. You can drown in a glass of water; you can drown in a puddle on the street.

I only felt soothed when I saw things through Constantine's eyes. The coach was the sole person who didn't get into the water. He stood safely on the shallow-end deck and watched the ceiling descend from the sky like a massive, down-floating projectile from another world. One moment, there were cries and the roar of water, then silence, all his swimmers vanishing beneath a landscape of grey stucco dunes, squat crater-lipped volcanoes and wire-like plants. All so beautiful, simple and still. Only a faint plaster-dust drifting in the air.

A week later the ground opened and again the roaring of water, my world imploding, an iron slab as wide as the ocean beating up and down on the top of my head.

A special post-trauma workshop paid for by the city. We sat in a square-like formation that I thought very much resembled a swimming pool and, one by one, described what we'd experienced. We were encouraged to be as graphic as possible. But as people spoke, I couldn't take my eyes from a black wire dangerously stapled to the wall and running up to a ceiling juncture that I was sure wasn't a right angle.

I heard things I never knew could happen. Some people in the shallow end who could touch bottom tried banging their heads against the barrier, broke through yet emerged with bloodied, swollen skulls. Tom, safely at the side and untouched by the fallen ceiling, dived under to rescue others, got lost in the dark and was trapped himself. A woman's goggles fell off, plaster filled her eyes and at the pool bottom she lost all sense of direction. Then the last-minute-of-life stories. Julia: 'I wanted to cry out, "I don't want it to happen like this, it's dark, nobody can see me."' The doctor in lane 3: 'I thought, of all the ways I'd ever considered going, this wasn't one of them.' Tony: 'I thought I had a choice and honestly wasn't sure I wanted to go on but decided, yes I would, and started bashing my head against the ceiling. I didn't care what happened to my body; I just wanted to get out.' Voices crescendoed in a chorus of wails, people sobbed, faces in hands, as terrified I watched a part of the cord where I was sure a live wire was exposed, a spark only had to touch the wallpaper and all our bruised bodies would be devoured by flames.

Then the doctor asked me what my name was and told me to tell my story. I shifted on the couch. Everyone seemed to be leaning forward. Was there no choice but to speak? Plaster specks whirled before my eyes.

'I got stuck,' I said, head lowered. 'I just got stuck.' The room was still, expectant. 'And there was a hole just off to my right. I didn't know it was there. There was no light coming through it.' I wondered why not and looking up, asked, 'Why was there no light?' My friends watched, listening. No light? A technical detail I now placed in my brain to ponder later. 'And there in the dark just briefly –' I squeezed my fingers and said it because I had to – 'I thought I

29

was dying.' I looked off to one side. 'That's what I thought.' Before my eyes, a murky darkness; somewhere, echoed rhythmic thuds. 'And my last thoughts were … Now I'm dying and all because I joined a stupid swim team.' Banalities. Banalities decide everything. Thankfully some swimmers tried to laugh. 'Then my parents who I never see –' Do I have to say this? I made myself do it. 'They popped into my mind and I thought, they'll never get over this. Their lives are ruined.' The rushing streams pulled the goggles from my eyes as my hands beat upwards like little wings while, below, my legs thrashed in empty space. Why had water always seemed so inno-cent? I bathed in it, washed my face in the morning, kept a glass of it beside my bed as a child, but in the trapped darkness it'd become hostile, an enemy pushing into my eyes-sockets, filling my mouth, sliding its fingers down my throat, descending slowly into my lungs. When my panic escalated to blind terror, every sentence in my head exploded into incomprehensible fragments and my brain dissolved, became like water whipping against the inside of my skull. 'And then suddenly I was above the water,' I said exhaling. 'I'd come up through a hole in the barrier.' All around there'd been a moonscape of grey stucco dunes, piles of jagged rocks on shore, above, a black sky of dangling wires. 'I can't recall any moment of transition though I guess there was one. I was just down and then I was up.'

The doctor finally said, 'Thank you,' and his words were like two iron doors closing. There was a ringing in my ears. From the end table I lifted my glass of Coke, took a drink.

One year later I received a cheque in the mail, and it was as if a wave washed over me, then receded. Safely on dry land for twelve months, I now stood very still in my metal-bright kitchen where drawers rose in perfect rows. I lowered myself to a chair that squeaked when I sat on it.

I studied the crisp, clean piece of uncrinkled paper. I flicked its sharp edge between my fingers. When I turned it around in the air, nothing happened, no dams exploded, no floods were unleashed. I stared at the number composed of fixed, precise zeros, each as hard as nuts that can be cracked between your teeth.

I am now in love with mathematics. $1+1 = 2$, $2+2 = 4$ ... is the simple refrain I use to get through the day. All the troubles of this world can be written on a piece of paper you carry in your pocket. I took mine to the bank and gave it to a man who stamped out a perfect rectangle full of parallel lines.

All around, water flows from taps, runs down pipes into sewers that lead into streams and into pipes and back again. When I try to hold something definite in my hands, it flows through my fingers and is gone. I still swim. I do the backstroke from one lane end to the other, studying the arches, crossbeams and lights of the pool's new ceiling. I know it as an astronomer knows the sky, or a botanist his plants, or I my own name. I look at the ceiling. I look at the sky. I look at my skin; I marvel at the thinness of this layer separating inside from outside.

Should I step outside my obsession? That would require trust which creates inattentiveness, and I could dissolve into a spray and cease to be a person completely. Paranoia holds you together and defines you more intensely than anything I've tried. If that pool ceiling hadn't fallen in, perhaps I'd have to knock it down myself.

Come walk the streets of my city of imperfect angles. Each year the change of seasons cracks the pavement and the ground trembles when a subway train passes below. Buildings are playing-card fortresses that will collapse if we exhale too suddenly. I know this is nothing to get upset about. Some things fall down but some stay up. Besides, we live in houses. Perhaps if we take it on faith, the wall you hang a picture on will stay standing. For a while anyway.

Laughing Forever

Monstrous, blood-webbed eyes, mauve pupils that stab and impale, the oblate nose obscenely moist, wound-red, emitting a deafeningly HONK when touched, the mouth lipless as a skeleton's, beige teeth flat as tombstones, the gaps between which fingers can be caught, shredded or severed, and no hair on the top of his head but, on the sides, heaps of poisonous, pink mould, his trumpet-mouthed ears full of hook-headed fuzz brittle as the hair on tarantula-legs.

'Hello, everybody, my name's Drooper!'

A shriek high as a tuning fork struck on concrete cut through the children's cheers, cries, laughter.

Mrs Freed pushed between the clapping, outstretched hands, her high heels clopping to the back of the class where Roy crouched beneath the craft table, his chest rising and falling, hands clutching the leg so tightly you'd almost swear you could hear wood cracking. Mrs Freed pried him loose and hurried him out into the hall, sat him on the tiled floor and said, 'Wait here for a while.'

The steady hum of the fluorescent light soothed him. He gazed at drawings hung along the wall like tea-towels in a quiet world without wind. Psychedelic sticks and squiggles danced from one end of the hall to the other. The solid, cool tile beneath his behind was reassuring. His breathing became steadier.

He could hear the circus music lilting like a man walking with a limp, the high-pitched accordion-whine like a baby crying. The laughter and shouts of students climbed and fell in waves. He made out the clown's voice, shrieking like a train whistle, bleating like a goat, belting out a grandiose vibrato like an opera singer.

He pressed his face to his knees. 'Don't get taken over,' he whispered out loud, thinking of his friends Murray, Tom, Sally. 'Don't let them take you over.'

The world was very big. The schoolyard fence was not the Earth's end; the ground went past it and continued on and on into the distance. Roy had seen the map on the classroom wall, learned about North America, South America, Asia, the vast uninhabited expanses on the world's surface, yet in the blank regions where nobody lived, in the empty spaces between towns, cities and highways, clowns, the invisible clowns, were dancing.

When the door handle clicked, Roy bolted to his feet and ran to the end of the hall.

Mrs Freed spoke haltingly. 'Are you sure you don't want to just talk to the clown, Roy? He's very friendly.'

Roy heard a voice, a crackling American accent, 'Hey pardner, don't be scared. I'm your friend.'

Roy raced down the L-wing, into the washroom, the cubicle, slammed shut and locked the door, sat on the john and put his feet up. He took the roll of toilet-paper, gleaming white and unbelievably soft, and pressed it against his face, closed his eyes.

I should wrap myself with this and become a mummy. That way if they find me, they'll think I'm dead, go away and leave me alone.

'He got scared of a clown?' Mark said.

'Be quiet. He'll hear you.'

'I hope he does hear me.'

'He's always been scared of them but he seems to have gotten worse.'

'Jesus Christ.'

Roy lay beneath the covers, listening in his bedroom.

Soon he got up, went to the kitchen for a glass of water.

Mark said, 'So Roy, I heard that at school today you acted like a girl.'

'Mark.'

'Are the other kids making fun of you, putting on clown noses and going "Boo." You know, if the guys on the hockey team ever find out, they'll give you a nickname just like they did that Spenser kid. "Mollyboy" or "Sissyspaz".'

'Mark, honestly.' Janey turned to Roy. 'Tonight we're having spaghetti and meatballs.'

'There you go pampering him again. That's not gonna help.'

Roy put the glass under the faucet and turned the handle.

Janey said quietly to Mark, 'He's picked up something loopy by being around your friends. They're the ones he should start laughing at.'

Laughter. Roy is the boy who never laughs. He hears people say that about him all the time.

'It's good for him to meet my friends, and you like it, don't you, Roy? Before, you were so small, and I couldn't have people over.' Then Mark said, 'We should take him to a circus. How about that, eh Roy?'

Janey said, 'Don't be ridiculous.'

'Roy, you'll like it. Lots of clowns and you'll see they're funny. A clown gets water sprayed down his pants and we laugh; he trips on his big shoes, his pants fall, he's got on flowered gotchies, it's hilarious –'

'Mom, I don't want to go to the circus.'

'Come on!' said Mark. 'You'll love it!'

'What's it matter if he's got some fears; he'll outgrow them. Fear is normal. I'm terrified of spiders. We all have irrational feelings.'

'My son doesn't.'

Janey put the plates on the table, the knives, the cups. She observed the steam hissing from the pot on the stove. She sat, ran one hand through her hair. Then she turned to Roy and said quietly, gently, 'Honey, why is it you don't like clowns? Why don't you tell me this time?'

Suddenly Roy felt he was at the bottom of the ocean. If he spoke, who would hear him? Words formed in his head that dissolved before he opened his mouth.

That night Roy lay in bed while his parents argued. When he finally fell asleep, he dreamt he was surrounded by a group of clowns that were hitting him with little paddles and laughing. They all started saying, 'Shake my hand,' 'Shake my hand,' and when he did, a vibrating metallic pin drilled into the tender palm of his hand again and again; they sprayed bottles of seltzer in his face and the hard, salty rods of liquid stung his lips, cheeks, nose, made his eyes burn, and when he stood up, his pants started falling down and each time he pulled them up they dropped and each time they dropped his underwear was more embarrassing, first having red-and-white stripes, then turning girlie-pink, next covered in tulip-bulbs and then little rabbits eating ice-cream. The clowns laughed and laughed holding their stomachs and falling to the ground, hysterically beating the pavement so hard with their fists that everything, the bungalow he lived in, the sidewalk, his backyard tree with the swing on it, started shaking and, when the earthquake finally happened, the street, houses, sidewalk, school and parking lot at the end of the road were ripped into a thousand concrete shards pointing in all directions at once. He called out his mother's name and was at the ocean-bottom surrounded by schools of fish wearing clown noses. When he tried to speak, his lips opened, water filled his mouth and one by one the laughing fish swam between his lips and down his throat.

He awoke trembling. He lay there for a moment, told himself to be calm. Looking about the dark silent room, he knew most of the clowns were still a long way off, though they were getting closer. He got up to go to the bathroom. As he passed the kitchen, out of the corner of his eye, he glimpsed his parents in the half-lit kitchen. They were pressed against each other, both naked; in one hand his father held a riding crop.

In the washroom, Roy's lips beneath the faucet, the cold, clean water rising from the centre of the Earth.

The next morning Mark shook him awake.

'C'mon, she's gone.'

Roy, bleary-eyed, was dressed, combed, fed.

'Let's go.'

It wasn't until Roy was in the car that he realized what was happening. 'No, I don't want to go!'

'Shush, shush.' Driving, Mark kept saying, 'Mom thinks she's such tough stuff,' and chuckling.

The circus tent rose like the huge pot-belly of a sleeping giant. Strings of blinking lights hung from the roof and tinfoil, sequined streamers blew in the wind. The empty parking lot was streaked with ribs of light and shadow.

'We're early,' said Mark. 'Do you want a donut?'

Roy stared at the dark, square entranceway, then at his smirking father.

'It's gonna be a great show,' he said, patting Roy's head.

As Mark led Roy in, the boy resisted, dug his feet in the red carpet, but the ground sloped downwards and the black doorway contained a magnetic force that drew him forward.

Throngs of adults and shouting children spun before him in a kaleidoscope.

Trumpets blared, and monkeys, a giraffe, flag-strewn elephants parading in a circle and then – about a half dozen, each completely bald, heads motley as stained, rancid heads of cauliflower, mouths like diagonal knife-slashes made in fetid, plasticine faces, all squealing so hysterically you couldn't tell if they were laughing or crying.

Roy wanted to control himself because if he didn't, his father would lose faith in him completely, but it was impossible; besides, with clowns, self-control sometimes harms you.

His scream was like a fire alarm Mark couldn't shut off. He covered Roy's mouth with his hand, his scarf, then embraced him. 'It's OK.' The sound sank its teeth into Mark's eardrums, seeped through the pores in his skin, penetrated his cartilage, his bone.

Roy knew his best defence was to let the fear flood his body, flow unrestricted through his lungs, throat, mouth. When he's undivided like this, the clowns cannot touch him.

Outside, Mark put down the exhausted boy. 'Geez, you're one fine cracker,' he said.

Roy lay in bed with a fever.

'So bloody arrogant.' Janey choked back tears. 'Right under my nose and I said no. I should be the one who knows how to deal with him. I see him more.'

Mark kept his head down.

Roy closed his eyes, knew the clowns were getting closer.

When he opened his eyes, the edges of his vision were cloudy as if somewhere, unseen, a clown had made a V with his index and third fingers and poked it into Roy's eyes, just as he'd once seen happen on *The Three Stooges*.

Roy listened to the wind beating at the windowpane, rattling the loose eavestrough. He recalled the map-covered walls of his classroom that daily surrounded him on all sides. He knew now that all across the vast, empty, wind-swept tundra of the million, jagged, jigsaw islands called the Northwest Territories, and down through harsh, impenetrable, rock-gouged forests and night-black lakes of the Canadian Shield, through the never-visited, wild wastes of Northern Alberta, Manitoba, Quebec, where wilderness stretched away on all sides seemingly forever, there, the clowns were crawling out of underground caves, emerging through damp, fern-lipped clefts in the earth, from behind thundering, boulder-rimmed waterfalls, and in the thousands, millions, were coming together and migrating south like packs of rabid wolves, moving closer to the city where Roy lived. The clowns he'd seen today and at school were testing the territory for the others. Next, the full-scale invasion.

When Roy fell asleep, he dreamt the clowns surrounded him. They leapt at him like dogs and bit out huge chunks of flesh.

Janey and Mark sat talking in low voices until Mark turned away and ran a hand across his forehead. 'Geez, if any of the guys at the loading dock find out my son's going to a head-shrinker!'

'There's no choice. He's gonna see clowns on TV or at school. Why should he have to be upset for no reason?'

Roy knew he was not like other boys. None of his friends had his fears. He sensed somewhere there was an exit door that could lead him out of terror but was beginning to realize he didn't want to use it. Was he a fool not to?

At night Roy again heard the metronome tick of his parents' bed hitting the wall, and he fell asleep amidst the sound of his mother's laughter like tinkling glass and his father repeating 'Foxy, foxy lady ...'

The next day Janey said, 'Roy, today we're going to take you to a nice lady who'll make you feel better.' Crouching, she ran a comb through his hair. 'You can tell her whatever you want – even about Dad and me. She only wants to help and hear if you have any problems.'

Travelling along Brown Street, Roy squinted out the car window, the breeze flicking at the bangs on his forehead. Stripes of light and shadow flew across his face. In the air was the smell of flowers, not regular flowers, but clown flowers. The smell was sickly sweet, like vanilla extract mixed with the scent of burnt cotton candy. The flowers were worn on the lapel and when you approached, they shot streams of sticky jelly or sour milk that stung your cheeks and made your eyes run.

The clowns were not so far away. The wind was now blowing from the North.

When they left the car, Janey said, 'What's that smell? Like roses but gross.'

Roy stared at her. She was starting to realize.

She pointed her wand-like key stick at the car and, click, everything magically closed.

Roy sat on the squeaky sofa and eyed Dr Rummel, a stout, buxom woman who, in her paisley jumper and bib, seemed an overgrown kid herself. Her glasses, iron-rimmed and hanging from a steel cord about her neck, were all that was adult about her.

The first session she asked him a lot of questions. 'How is school?' 'What's your favourite subject?' 'Who's your best friend?' 'Why?' She smiled a lot and nodded her head, said 'Oooh' and 'Aaah' even after things Roy didn't think were that interesting.

'I've heard that you never laugh. Not at all. Your mother told me. Well, if you want to laugh in my office, Roy, feel free. Here you can just let 'er rip.'

Roy knew he would never do that because laughter was dangerous. Laughs had to be given sparingly and for a short duration of time. If you open your mouth too wide, just once, you don't know what will come out of it.

Finally Dr Rummel said, 'You did really good today, Roy. I'm glad you came.'

After, Mark said, 'So what's wrong?'

'I need more time for observation.'

Mark wanted to say, 'At what you get paid, I'd think you'd observe faster,' but instead fell into the gloomy silence that had overtaken him lately.

Soon Dr Rummel let Roy play in the toy-room full of GI Joes, Barbies, Terminators and plastic dogs and cows. She occasionally wrote things on her elastic-bound clipboard.

One day she put a five-centimetre-long plastic clown in the play area. When Roy saw it, he took a deep breath, stared at it, then grabbed and hurled it to the other side of the room. The next few sessions Dr Rummel brought other clowns, and Roy responded the same way.

'We're making progress,' she said to his parents. 'He keeps throwing the clowns away. This clearly gives him a feeling of power over his life so he can fight whatever the clown represents.'

Mark was ecstatic. That night he bought a video, *Barnum and Bailey Circus Clowns*.

'Hey Roy, let's see how much fun you can have now.'

'Mark, I don't think –'

'Come on.'

Bozo's face flashed on the screen and Roy began screaming.

Mark yelled, 'She gets paid for what? For what?'

Finally at the eighth session Dr Rummel was speaking to Roy and suddenly interrupted with a comment designed to sneak past his willed, judgment-inducing, conscious mechanisms and unearth whatever was hidden below. 'Er, clowns, Roy, you hate 'em. Why?'

Roy looked away, again felt he was in empty space reaching for words that dissolved when touched. He took the plastic Geronimo and moved his legs so he was walking across the bridge.

Dr Rummel sat quiet, unmoving. Clearly, this would be one of those serious days, no games but a barrage of questions.

'I was thinking,' her eyes shifted upwards, 'about the clowns' bodies. You don't like them. Is there something about their bodies you don't like?'

He shrugged. Geronimo was now standing in the middle of the bridge.

Roy knew that Dr Rummel had a lot of patients. There was a boy with shiny, square glasses who came before him and a limping, red-haired girl afterwards. What if Dr Rummel could magically make the clowns disappear from the Earth? What if he allowed her to free him? No, he thought, no. Too risky. If they return when you don't expect them, it's worse than when they arrive and you know they're coming.

Dr Rummel asked, 'Roy, how would you describe these clowns?'

He stared ahead, thought for a minute. Then he said, 'Creepy.'

'Creepy,' she said, 'as in, they'll creep all over you?' She picked up the Peter Pan doll. 'I'll tell you a true story. Once there was a boy like this boy and there was a ... man.' She carefully lifted Bozo. 'A clown who did very bad things to the boy. The boy felt very sad. He wouldn't tell anyone about it because the boy thought he him-self was bad. But who was wrong, the boy or the clown?' Roy watched silently. 'Who?' she repeated gently. He didn't answer. 'The clown was wrong,' she said, 'not the boy.' Exasperated, Dr Rummel at last said, 'Roy, has anyone ever touched you ... in a way you didn't like?'

He reflected. 'Once Murray hit me.'

'Only then? Did anyone else touch you ... in a bad way? Did a clown ever touch you?'

Roy pondered.

'No.'

'Really? Did you ever get close to a clown? Did you always run away from them?'

Had he ever actually spoken to a clown? Of course not. He wasn't crazy.

Dr Rummel collapsed back into her chair. 'I'm your friend, Roy. I'm here to help you. You know you can tell me whatever you want.'

If he could allow himself to follow the path Dr Rummel gestured towards. If he could put one foot on its shiny bricks and walk. No. He was sure he'd lose something. But what?

He placed Geronimo on the tractor, drove him back and forth, back and forth.

Dr Rummel told his parents she'd have to try a behavioural approach because the analytic sessions weren't working.

That afternoon Roy walked slowly about the playground, past the line of noisy children waiting to get on the slide, the kids screaming on the whirly-spinner, listened to people shouting on the swings. From the top of the domed metal scaffolding of the monkey bars, a boy sang, 'I'm the king of the castle and you're the dirty rascal.' The girls played hopscotch, jumpsies and double dutch, 'Lento – jolio – peppers,' while the younger kids drove Tonka trucks about the octagonal sandbox. He heard two older boys talking: 'Did you hear about the Newfie who said "No"?' 'No.' 'You're the Newfie.'

Soon all this would be wiped out. Now the clowns were camped out, just on the edge of the city, living in makeshift tents that protected them from the rain, wind and sudden drop of temperature at night.

Just above the distant hill Roy could make out the pointed roofs, the occasional outline of a faraway figure with a hairdo round as a basketball, or wearing a long, narrow hat, sometimes shaped like oil tanks or the Eiffel Tower upside down.

At night in the darkness he could hear chuckling coming from the distance. His father came in, turned on the light and said, 'Who's making that racket,' and Roy pointed out the window.

His father marched to the window, flipped open the blind and stared into the dark, his brow creased.

Roy could see everyone was changing. His mother was putting on makeup every day as well as gaudy lipstick as red as a fire engine. Turning to him, she said, 'Do you think it makes me look happier when I wear this?'

The air on the street was saturated with the smell of burnt candy floss. People stood coughing in doorways, and Roy saw an old lady who had to be wheeled indoors.

Roy dreamt he was trapped in the rotating funhouse barrel; no matter how fast he moved his feet from one side to the other he couldn't get off; at one point, exhausted, he collapsed, yet the barrel kept moving until he hung upside down in the air. Then he was lost in Bozo's House of Glass, desperately trying to find his real reflection in the ceiling-high mirrors, but he was always distorted, his forehead triangular, his chin pencil-thin, or his chest wide and rectangular beneath a Popsicle-stick head; in some his teeth were as large as a rabbit's, in others his eyeballs covered his whole face, while his ears stuck out like parking meters, and when he finally crashed through a pane of glass and was out in the midway, everyone, including his father and mother, were either short as dwarves with enormous square feet that clanked on the ground like toppled mailboxes, or had torsos curled like croissants, or heads shaped like hourglasses, or gigantic, bulbous behinds that went from their ankles to their necks and farted in your face when you got near.

Roy awoke breathing heavily. He ran his hands over his body to make sure it was still all there.

The next day Mrs Freed had to close the classroom windows because of the noise, shouts, screams, the sound of clapping hands and accordion music coming from beyond the nearby hill.

With the windows closed you could still hear it, so Roy tried to concentrate on the blackboard: $7 \times 2 = 14$, $8 \times 2 = 16$, yet he knew he could fill his head with every number in the world but the change to come was unavoidable.

Still, Roy realized that somewhere there was a borderline between himself and the outside world and he could move it closer or farther away, according to how he felt. He sensed he was standing on the threshold of something perhaps not totally awful, but what it was exactly, he didn't know.

As he walked home, the street was silent. Birds called gently from one tree to another. A lone car crawled past, its dangling muffler scratching faded exclamation-marks in the pavement. Roy scrutinized the faraway hill, which now, just for a moment, appeared to contain only trees, rocks and grass.

When he entered the house, his mother and father were seated quietly at the kitchen table.

After dinner Janey said, 'Roy, we were talking to Dr Rummel and she's asked us to do something special that may help you.'

She looked at Mark who sighed. 'She wants me to dress up like a bloody clown.'

'She says it will help if you watch Daddy put on a clown costume. You'll see clowns are just normal people like everybody else and there's nothing to be afraid of.' She carefully put a heavy shopping bag on the table. Watching Roy, she slowly took out a polka-dot clown suit, rubber nose, wig and floppy shoes, and laid them before him. 'See, Roy, they're just clothes.'

Roy said nothing but stared. At one point he reached out and briefly put one finger on the spotted nylon pants.

Janey said, 'Now, Dad can put it on.'

Mark took off his shirt, shoes, pants, put one leg, then the other into the speckled suit. When he got his arms through the ruffled sleeves, Janey stood behind him and clipped shut the clasp.

'Now for the makeup,' said Janey.

She opened the little jars of red, blue, white, green facepaint. She used blue as a base and painted large red circles on his cheeks, white spheres around his eyes, a green oval encircling his mouth. She told Mark to put on the wig.

'How do we use the shoes?' Janey said.

They discovered they could be easily slipped over Mark's bare feet.

He stood up, looked at Roy and, trying to smile said, 'What do you think of your old dad now?'

Roy just watched.

'Mark, you should do a little dance,' said Janey. 'Move your hands in the air and stomp your feet.'

Leaping, Mark swung one hand in the air. He stopped. 'I feel like a bloody homo,' he said.

Roy was silent.

'What's this?' said Janey. She discovered a water-pistol at the bottom of the bag. She filled it with water from the sink, held it before Mark's face and squeezed the trigger once. Water struck his cheek and suddenly, miraculously, the room seemed to fill with light, as Roy smiled.

Janey squirted her husband again and again as Mark danced faster, and Roy's grin grew wider and wider. Soon his father's face was completely wet, the red face-paints flowing onto his polka-dot chest. Janey opened the kitchen fridge, took the remainder of the Sara Lee pie they'd just had for dessert and smushed it in Mark's face. Roy let out what sounded vaguely – like a titter. Or was it? Janey snatched a carton of eggs from the fridge, opened it and broke one on Mark's forehead, one against his cheek, then she put two on the chair and Mark sat on them. She said, 'Mark, pretend it's an apple', and Mark said, 'Oh, look at this delicious white apple' and bit into the side of it. The yolk dribbled down his chin as he spit out bits of eggshell.

Roy clapped his hands together. 'Ha!' he said.

His parents looked at each other. Mark grabbed his son's hand, said, 'C'mere, Roy!' rushed him into the living room. He clicked a video into the slot, smearing whipped cream on both the volume dial and the ON button, and when Bozo's smiling face appeared on the screen, Roy began to cry. Large tears of loss rolled down his cheeks.

Mark stared in disbelief. Then he shouted, 'Jesus fucking Christ!' removed and flung the wig to the ground, reached behind to undo the costume, tore it off in one swift movement and stormed upstairs.

Janey cried out, 'Oh Mark, please, honey, Mark.' She pressed the VIDEO OFF button and ran upstairs after him.

Roy sat quietly staring at the abandoned clown costume.

He wouldn't cry ever again. He had finally decided. This was the last time.

As he'd watched himself crying, just as he'd lately watched himself eating, walking, doing homework, he realized certain things were inevitable and that obvious, large-scale invasions upstage subtler ones and prevent the hidden catastrophes taking place daily amongst billions of people beyond this house, the schoolyard, the ravine-gouged edge of this small suburb. Only terror can hold in place the frayed parts of this too-changing life. If clowns disappeared from the world, would there be anything left of Roy? He repeated a phrase Dr Rummel often used: 'Certainly not.'

A flood of peace rolled through him. He felt his muscles relax, his breath deepening – but only for a moment.

What would ever become of him? A part of Roy, just recently born, wanted to find out.

He knew the time had come. A disguise could save him. Temporarily.

Overhead he heard the rhythmic pounding of his parents' bed against the wall and the whole house began to shake, somewhere a huge fist was beating the ground and when he rose and looked out the window, he saw the entire street was trembling, trees starting to fall. He could be safe from them only if he was like them. He slowly put one foot, then the other into the polka-dot costume, lifted it over his shoulders, reached behind, snapped the clasp shut. The suit was big, allowing him still a bit of growing room if he needed it. He slapped on the leftover paint; it didn't matter how it looked, just as long as it hid the fact he'd been crying. The pounding intensified. Quivering yet trying to ignore his fear, he stepped carefully down the stairs to the side door, put his hand on the knob, turned, opened, stepped through the doorway.

He stood on the street. The pounding had stopped.

He inhaled very deeply.

Then It happens:

A rising roar of clamorous shouts, hoots, shrieks, shrill accordion music, applause like rain on pavement, a sing-song 'Dog-gie DAAW-GEE', as on the distant hill a multicoloured wave rises up and over, descends, and from the south, north, west, east, teeming, riotous, chaotic crowds of leaping, bouncing, crawling, cartwheeling clowns. Their hair juts like helicopter blades, their protruding tongues wag like dogs' tails. They swarm forward across the roads, sidewalks, lawns, flow up onto bungalow roofs, where they scale chimneys and TV aerials. They scream through bullhorns, wave signs reading GUFFAW GUFFAW, dance in speckled undies, hit each other with huge rubber hammers, run races on their hands screeching all the way, swim in puddles of water an inch deep, blow gigantic police-whistles in each other's ears, roll back and forth through pools of sparkly paint, strike two-by-fours against each other's behinds that then honk like cars in traffic; they dump pots of sludge-coated spaghetti on each other's heads, pull unending strings of elastic snot from their noses, douse each other with buckets of tomato soup, chocolate milk, and confetti. Wearing floppy shoes and ballerina tutus they prance in ridiculous circles, blow kisses from atop bungalow awnings or telephone poles or while hanging from hydro wires. Suddenly they all pull out a billion whoopee cushions, sit and the whole world farts at once – and then in the sky, a huge whirling fan appears sending forth a blinding storm of shredded tissue paper, inundating the formless, tumultuous multitude; paper fragments slap Roy's face, get in his eyes, hair, mouth, the sun has become a strobe light flashing, someone blows a horn in Roy's ear, rips off his Velcro-seamed pants to reveal floral undies and a neon sign flashing 'Kick me', takes his hand and together they dance, spinning round and round and, in Roy's gut, a sound forms, part shriek, part wail, part bellow, that rises up through his throat, mouth, between his lips to merge perfectly with the outside world, a long, lasting sound of defiant, pain-fraught, triumphant and obscene laughter.

Believing in Paris

When I took Claude with me to Paris, I had no idea it'd be his last trip. Would I have invited him if I'd known the truth? I like to think so but am not sure. This is not a morality tale meant to showcase ethically right and wrong actions and their effects on the larger world. Claude was too complex to put in one slot and I no longer feel I know how to judge anything. The fact is that when we boarded the Air France plane in Toronto, he'd already contracted HIV and was well into the final stages of full-blown AIDS; already his kidneys had stopped functioning and there were multiple tumours on his liver and spleen; yet, as is the terrible irony of his disease, he looked perfectly healthy. To me anyway. No one knew the secret that Claude carried about and carefully guarded except for an anonymous clinic doctor who'd said, 'Take these pills and your shingles will go away; by the way you've got HIV,' eight years ago, in the early days of the disease when people didn't know if compassion was permitted. Why Claude never confided in me is a question I can never answer. Did he think I'd be appalled? That I'd judge and reject him? Was he that ashamed? Why would he feel shame with me, and why does every question about Claude lead to another question and why do they all unleash such a torrent of anger?

A week after his death I sat stiffly at my parents' kitchen table as my mother said grace over the casserole. My parents feel that homosexuality is, if not sinful, undesirable and AIDS a punishment, if not for evil, then for foolhardiness. As I moved my fork in circles through the mix of hamburger, carrots, mashed potatoes and peas, I kept thinking, should I tell them what happened to the quiet young man my father had so kindly driven to the airport? Should I throw this boulder on the table?

Unfortunately, when all the details of Claude's life at last became public, even people who loved him concluded he should've died sooner. Sometimes I wonder why I had him as a friend in the first place. Why did our friendship last so long, and why did I invite

49

him, of all people, to come with me to Paris?

Already in the airport lounge he'd started complaining.

'You probably didn't book the right plane; you always screw things up.'

'Air France is late; airlines are often late.'

'You should've booked another one.'

I'd had to do all the bookings as Claude was dyslexic and couldn't read – another one of his secrets, but this one he'd told me about. Perhaps that was why I assumed he'd tell me everything else.

When the loudspeaker announced the boarding, Claude quieted down, and later, as we walked through the wind-rattled boarding bridge, he moved silently, his head lowered, saying nothing. He wasn't afraid of flying but was nervous about going to unfamiliar places. Still, he'd been overjoyed when I'd suggested he accompany me to Paris. 'It'd be a dream to go there!' He'd hardly travelled anywhere.

He carried a large shopping bag full of bottles of Italian cologne he'd just bought at the duty-free, not for Paris, 'But later,' he'd said, 'Delorial at $70 is a good deal.'

Once seated in the plane's stiff orange seats, I reached ahead into the bulging pocket full of shining in-flight magazines. We were going to Paris, actually going to Paris. I was glad Claude was here because if alone, I would have felt stressed. I played with the plastic tray supported by two aluminium bars, clicked it shut, let it fall open, repeatedly collapsing and uncollapsing it. In just eight hours we'd be having croissants and *café au lait* at a sidewalk café as a street musician serenaded us with Edith Piaf tunes on his accordion.

A tall, thin flight attendant with a moustache and a blond streak in his hair stood before us and pretended to pull a life-saver cord as a bilingual voice-over explained evacuation procedures.

I said to Claude, 'The steward's really cute.'

Claude grinned at him and said slyly, 'I know.'

Between my legs I clutched my dictionary and exercise book. I'd taken a month-long French course in preparation for my trip. I loved speaking a language that wasn't my own. The words seemed to lack the weight they had in English and I felt I were speaking in code, as if what I was saying wasn't real and I couldn't be held responsible for anything. The Parisians, unlike the Québecois, who annoyingly switch into English as soon as they hear my accent, would respond in their own language, thus keeping me safely enmeshed in what seemed a dream world.

I'd invited Claude along partly because he was the only francophone I knew. He'd be a bridge between me and France. Yet he usually refused to speak French with me because I had such trouble deciphering his northern Ontario accent. 'I'd have to use baby talk for you to understand.'

The flight lights flashed.

'Put on your seat belt, Claude.'

And then it happened: a rumbling throughout the plane as, outside, the pavement stripes blurred together, the entire cabin slanted skyward, the thud of the retracting landing gear like the slam of a door locking out the past forever – we were in the air, heading towards Paris, the City of Dreams. I felt I'd burst through an invisible yet very real barrier that had surrounded me on all sides, imprisoning me in Toronto, where I lived in a matchbox-sized apartment and worked at a job I disliked. I taught English to rich, spoiled tourists with whom I had to be ever servile and ingratiating. I was embarrassingly underpaid, yet it was 1995 and the recession had created an employer's market. I simply couldn't find another job; so I spent much of my free time in coffee shops and bars searching for a boyfriend who'd make me forget my frustrations. Months passed, years passed and I was perennially single without knowing why. Surely people could sense my desperation. In France none of this would matter. It was my turn to be in an unknown place where I could now revel in the unbridgeable differences between myself and the world around me.

Claude peered out over the passing fields, the white-blue coast of Lake Ontario. It was his first time in a plane and I'd thought the trip would be a treat for him; I really was curious to see how he'd react to everything: flights, landings, Europe. It was hard to even imagine him there. How would his ability to charm play itself out in France? He knew little about Europe and so could only go where I'd take him, which suited me.

Claude turned back from the window, his face expressionless.

When dinner was served, he flirted with our flight attendant, as expected. This was his special skill. 'I guess you've been slicing up vegetables all day,' he said. Claude's banter was innocent, inoffensive and frivolous, something I can't mimic. Whenever I meet someone, I get too intense and knotted up inside, as if my every sentence were deathly important and the world would come crashing down if I put one word in the wrong place. Numerous times in bars, at parties, Claude came and carelessly swooped away the person I was talking with.

After dinner, coming back from the washroom, Claude discovered the fridge where they stored the paid-for drinks and chips. Of course, he stole several. He arrived at my seat, laughing. His face was lit up, one of his eyebrows raised comically.

'Oh, Claude,' I said as he stuffed the booty in his backpack.

'You should go get some. They're free.' He smiled and warmly touched my shoulder.

Soon I found an Air France comment card in the pocket in front of me. I took out a pen and said, 'How about we write, "Nice flight attendant"? Here where it asks about uniforms – "Our guy would be better naked."' We both laughed out loud, trying to cover our mouths.

Claude said, 'You should just draw a dirty picture in the comment box.' We laughed again; Claude turned and, bemused, glanced up at the ceiling.

Was this why I had Claude as a friend? For these moments of fun?

I can picture the exterior of the plane: the straight red stripes running along the sides, the symmetrical nose-tip and wings level and perfectly identical, the plane balanced hovering in the empty void between cloud and outer atmosphere. I see myself sitting beside Claude, teaching him to play cards, no more aware of him than of the fathomless expanse outside our pin-prick windows. 'The ace is worth more than the numbered cards,' I said, staring at the pinched-lipped face of the Queen of Spades, the stern frown of the King, each surrounded by a red, round-cornered rectangle that seemed to contain the beginning and end of everything.

I only realized how little I knew of this man sitting next to me, later, much later – at his funeral in fact, where I heard many things for the first time: how Claude had left an abusive family when he was fourteen and lived for some years as a vagabond, surviving by forging cheques; how before he was twenty, he'd fathered two children who are now living in Kapuskasing. At the funeral parlour there were dozens of people I'd never seen before or even heard of. Where did he get so many friends and what had made him so popular? I only knew him as a high-strung nursing assistant who'd accompany me to bars where he'd complain about being single and how hard it was to get sex, though he seemed to get plenty. I can't find any connection between his troubled past and the man I knew, with his over-refined love of perfume and jewellery, his collection of elaborate, bulging amethysts, his apartment where I sat on a stiff-backed, chiffon-rimmed chair before a kidney glass coffee table as he said to me, 'Don't you go touching anything. You're like a little kid always moving things out of place.'

On our first day in Paris, Claude had never seemed so lost. He gazed wide-eyed down crowded, stone-walled streets, stared blankly at flashing signs he couldn't understand, though they were in his mother tongue. He breathed deeply as we walked through labyrinthine subway tunnels whose twists and turns were too irregular to memorize.

I could barely contain my happiness. I practically ran from one cobbled road to another, past intricately spired cathedrals that appeared from behind corners like hallucinations, down twisting, serpentine alleys that opened miraculously into tree-rimmed squares containing giant basins where water showered over half-naked stone mermaids. We went onward along sidewalks bustling with women in shin-length trousers, handkerchiefs worn round their necks with precise carelessness, men clothed in horizontal-striped shirts beneath Italian suit jackets, people I could never dress like, could never be like; on and on we continued past storefronts that changed abruptly from windows full of moisture-beaded kumquats and kiwis to sober rows of baguettes lined up like artillery, to patisserie displays of rippling, tusk-shaped meringues, choco-cubes glittering like solidified tar arranged in precise, geometric patterns. Two shopkeepers stood shouting at each other, a moustached woman wearing a top hat sang, 'Je ne regrette rien', a fire-breather in a psychedelic headband spit a flame above our heads. Nothing in this city seemed real. We skipped over the famous clear water flowing beneath Peugeots parked akimbo along the sidewalk curb and then – alleys full of cafés where ladies in triangle-lensed sunglasses, and old men in wonderfully clichéd berets sat reading books or holding cigarettes over disc-top tables with striped, wood-post legs; a silent sea of mannequins making the vague gestures of the barely human, as bow-tied waiters flew back and forth like frenzied paper marionettes caught in turbulent winds that would never stop blowing.

I spoke constantly to Claude, explaining everything, but I was really speaking to release my new energy.

We continued down lanes, across squares, through parkettes, in and out of bazaars, through clouds smelling of cologne, diesel fumes, baked bread. It seemed you could never get to the very centre of the city, as its maze-like streets led to worlds within worlds, and I thought if I were here a lifetime I would never know every crack and crevice but could insatiably devour newness every day. I spoke French as much as I could, asking people for directions when I didn't care where I was going, requesting menu suggestions from maître d's when the last thing I wanted to do was sit. When people tossed back snide, curt comments, I didn't care; their language wasn't real, it was all play, a wonderful game in which nothing could hurt me.

At noon I realized I hadn't thought of my Toronto life for five hours and felt proud of myself.

We had lunch in a brasserie. Claude ordered sausages. I wanted ham or chicken or cheese in a croissant, anything in a croissant. And an espresso for dessert.

Claude sat silently across from me, gazing over my shoulder. Occasionally he'd glance timidly to one side. He'd hardly spoken all morning. He ate his sausage in very slow, deliberate bites. Leaning forward he quietly asked me how much it all cost. When I said, 'About twelve dollars,' he just closed his eyes.

I loved watching the overweight waiter running about and making change from the money in his apron, peremptorily charging behind the back booth for no apparent reason. The sunlight reflecting on the silver-rimmed table hurt my eyes and I needed sleep. I read the foods on the chalkboard, trying to see how many I could translate.

'Claude, what's *espadon* mean?'

In a daze, not looking at me, he said 'I don't know.' He folded his hands carefully on the table before him.

If I'd looked closely, I would have noticed that a peculiar rash had started up on his forehead, destroying the hair follicles, causing his hairline to recede. As Claude sat in the restaurant, was he thinking about his illness?

He stared ahead in a stunned torpor induced by fatigue, jet lag, culture shock, and what else? His characteristic smile wouldn't light. He was too tired to joke with the waiter.

He came to when we had to pay the bill.

'It's very expensive,' he said.

'I told you the exchange rate is bad for us. You just have to accept it.'

Though Claude spent tons of money on things like jewellery, he hated paying for food or transportation, transitory things that left you with nothing concrete.

I used his own argument to make amends for our less-than-luxurious hotel room. When I first saw the room with its sagging beds, cracked wall mirror, the shower on another floor, I was afraid Claude would have a fit, but when I told him it was the cheapest and why waste money on accommodation, he seemed satisfied.

The next morning after having slept fourteen hours, we both woke refreshed and energized. I soon discovered that Claude's aggressive cockiness, which fear had tamed and subdued the day before, had returned with force and fury.

It all started at breakfast when he thought the restaurant menu prices were too high. After wandering for an hour and looking at dozens of sidewalk boards, we finally had to go to a *supermarché* to buy bread, cheese and orange juice to eat on a bench somewhere. I'd been looking forward to having a café au lait on a terrasse. We couldn't find any parks and were forced to sit and eat on the edge of a fountain like, I thought, tacky American tourists. Embarrassed I drank from a tin can, crumbs falling down my shirt.

Afterwards I took Claude to la Cathédrale Notre Dame.

He said, 'What are you doing walking so fast; this isn't a race.'

We stood in a square crowded with pointing tourists, screeching pigeons and vendors shouting, '*Sandwiches au jambon, Coca.*' Claude was impressed by the sheer size of the cathedral's beige, rectangular stone face bordered by two towers standing like immense, upended dominoes. I contemplated the whirling stained-glass windows below the row of stern-faced, gesturing apostles. In my guidebook there were photos of goblins that crouched on all fours, their tongues flicking like little knives, but I searched the cathedral's front and couldn't see them anywhere.

Claude asked me to take a picture of him. I remember his face in the frame: eyes half-closed, his large, broad grin backdropped against the colossal, sombre stone tower on one half of the photo and a cloudless, insanely blue sky on the other.

Soon we passed beneath the flapping banner proclaiming *L'Année de la Conception,* and were in the dark, dank interior. Though pink and blue light flooded the huge room, the fetid walls and wide, obstructing pillars made me feel I was in a subterranean cavern far underground. The swollen shadows of candleflames flickered hauntingly, the incense-laden air full of vague, echoing voices; somewhere the sound of water trickled. We sat in a pew, the rectangular back jutting into our shoulder blades.

After a few minutes Claude and I got into an argument. He wanted to go the front where people crouched before what he thought a very campy statue of a crowned Mary with hooker-red lipstick holding a silver box that looked like a toaster.

I said, 'It's disrespectful. Look, there are signs saying, No Photos.'

'They can't see me. And if they do, who cares? They don't know who I am.' He smiled his contagious smile, but I refused to smile back. I quickly launched into a condescending speech full of historical references and cultural analysis, intimidating him through his implied lack of knowledge until he reluctantly agreed to accompany me out of the cathedral.

Back on the street I said we'd go to Sacré-Coeur.

'What's that?'

'Another church.'

Claude exploded. 'We were just in one. Why do you want to go to another? You're not even Catholic.'

I began to realize that before now I'd only ever dealt with Claude in small doses, short evenings where any sudden irateness could be easily contained and controlled.

I eventually persuaded him to go to Sacré-Coeur by saying that we'd see some interesting things on the way, streets with paintings on display, a statue in a square, 'and Pigalle, the sex area.'

Claude's face brightened. 'Wow.' He laughed. 'That'd be fun.' He made a little playful leap in the air, and standing beside me, reached and squeezed my hand.

Together we started up the hill leading to Montparnasse and the red-light district.

Though dying and infected with sexually transmitted disease, Claude's favourite form of recreation was still sex.

Does it sound as if I'm judging him? I don't want to. I would rather Claude existed in a special realm outside the Judeo-Christian categories my religious upbringing has carved into my brain. But it's so hard to resist the desire to judge, pigeonhole, categorize. Of course I would never blame him for having AIDS; safe sex didn't exist when he contracted HIV and small mistakes do not make people evil. But it's difficult to recount what I subsequently learned of Claude without coming down firmly on one side or the other. I know my parents would judge him instantaneously.

Later at their kitchen table I sat staring into the hamburger meat, peas, broccoli heads, carrot slices swirling up and over one another, in and out of an ochre sauce that steamed incessantly as my mother talked of Uncle Jim's operation, the new pastor at the church … Sometimes it seems my life has always taken place on a silent, merciless, moral grid, a right-wrong checkerboard whose intersecting lines are relentless, steel-solid and razor-sharp. I cannot lift my eyes from the ground and if I could, I'm sure the air would be full of lines too. In my mother's glossy magazines there are articles about people living with AIDS who indiscriminately infect others. Didn't Preston Manning once call for a ban on people with HIV entering Canada? As I write these words, I want to say, look, Claude is not typical, and I don't know why I am publicizing his case. Should I shut up now? Am I being bad?

During the eulogy at Claude's funeral the priest said, 'It is tragic that so many young folk have died because of HIV.' Afterwards some mourners approached and accused him of making false statements. Confused, he turned to the older, bearded man he'd consulted with about the funeral and who'd been one of Claude's secret boyfriends. When the man said, 'Yes, Claude died of AIDS-related illness. Dr Finstein has confirmed this,' it was as if an electric shock went through the crowd. Some people there had been Claude's lovers for extended periods of time; I know of three who were regular 'fuck-buddies'. Apparently Claude had always refused to have sex safely because 'I'm clean, so if the other person isn't, it's his job to rubber himself.' My friend Bill once said, 'Claude always chose the nicest, the most innocent, inexperienced boys.' Sometimes Claude would point someone out in a crowd and cruelly say, 'He's got AIDS; you can tell by how he walks,' and he once told me he dumped a guy because he heard the guy was infected. How could he lie so unself-consciously and keep up such a polished act? Or did Claude not feel he was lying? Was the truth simply too troublesome? Can I find some uninterseting line outside the moral grid?

We never got to Sacré-Coeur as Claude got waylaid on the way, and we spent the afternoon in sleazy porno shops. He laughed as he flipped through magazines showing women having sex with pigs, a man sucking a horse, people eating shit, photos of gay sex more graphic than we were allowed to see in Canada. He wanted to go into the live-sex clubs until I told him they were expensive. He grimaced and pretended to sigh dramatically. I can't say I disliked our afternoon. My conception of Paris as an unreal, liberating city again surfaced as I realized I was having an experience not possible in Toronto.

Exiting onto rue Marbeuf I finally saw, in the distance, unbelievably, the Arc de Triomphe.

I began walking rapidly; Claude followed me. The best thing of all: we had to walk along the most famous street in the world, the Champs-Elysées. Everywhere were flashing lights, posh, luxury shops displaying designer suits, fur coats, gold-jewelled watches, and sprawling outdoor restaurants bustling beneath expansive, fringed canopies. We passed windows of impeccably dressed mannequins frozen in the most affected poses of snobbery imaginable, their heads held high, wrists bent elegantly. We squeezed by block-long lineups of people outside cinemas; I saw a billboard that showed a woman clubbing a man in the head with the Eiffel Tower. The streams of people thickened, flowed at a faster pace; as we ascended the hill, cars honked louder, lights flashed brighter as Claude grew weaker by the second. The adrenalin that the shock of arrival in France had caused to surge through his system could no longer energize his dying body. His head drooped, his feet shuffled along the sidewalk. I glanced at his pale face and assumed he was still jet-lagged.

Straight ahead, at the summit of the hill stood the magnificent stone arch that each second grew larger. I could soon make out the black, rearing stallions pulling the carts on the top. At last we stood on the edge of an eight-lane-wide stream of traffic that roared round the island containing the Arc. I turned to Claude and said, 'We'll run across. Be careful you don't get hit.' I leaped into the first lane, dodged a car, Claude stumbled drunkenly behind me, I crossed lanes

2, 3, 4, and amidst the honking cars and overpowering smell of diesel fuel, I sprinted across 5, 6, 7, 8, and was at the base of the Arc. I turned, Claude hobbled onto the island panting; from this height I could see the whole city that spun round on all sides, as just above my head, the night-black stallions galloped on towards victory.

Claude was standing still with his eyes closed. Then he opened them. He breathed in and out slowly, very slowly.

He turned to me and said something. I didn't understand.

'What?' I said.

'I shit myself.' I stared at his face, still not comprehending. 'I got shit in my pants.'

He shit himself. On the Champs-Elysées. I repeated the words in my head, not believing. Claude shit his pants on the Champs-Elysées? Claude shit himself on the Champs-Elysées. How could he do such a thing? Suddenly the stallions, the Arc, the entire whirling, glorious, wonder-filled city collapsed, and my mind shrank to accommodate this humiliation.

Now we had a practical problem: what were we going to do with Claude's shit?

Luckily there was a washroom at the base of the arc.

I waited outside. A few feet away, an old man in a kimono stood playing a saxophone.

Ten minutes later Claude returned. He said, 'When I was cleaning myself, some guy started banging on the door and shouting. By his voice I could tell he was a stupid Paki so I told him to get lost.'

On the north side we discovered a pedestrian walkway. We crossed over and followed the downward-sloping street to our hotel. I didn't speak to Claude all the way. For the first time I consciously regretted bringing him here.

Claude bought a bottle of water, drank some, wanted to store the container in my backpack.

'No, it'll rip the seams,' I said peevishly.

'Oh c'mon, you're just being difficult.'

Back in the hotel room I lay on my bed, silent. Claude was changing his clothes. I turned, saw his lightly-muscled chest, his slender thighs. He looked a bit thinner than usual. I assumed he hadn't been going to the gym enough.

A week after he died, I became obsessed with my own body. I stood before the mirror fondling my neck, the skin below my jaw, my chest muscles, testes, searching for swelling or discolouration. Did I have a sore throat? Though I knew the disease couldn't be transmitted through casual contact, I was ashamed to find I kept thinking about the water glass we'd shared in the hotel room, the toilet seat we'd both sat on, and years ago, so far in the past, the memory is a mere pencil-sketch with the important details missing, we'd had sex. Just once.

It was a few months after I'd 'come out'. I'd just recently started going to bars when he saw me, approached and began talking. He was friendly and fun and was delighted by my naivety. I openly asked him questions about the gay world, the best places to go, how to meet guys and even how to avoid AIDS. Rock Hudson had just died and I was terrified of the disease. When I asked him why he'd moved to Toronto, his eyes twinkled and he said coyly, 'To be with you.' I don't know if Claude was infected at the time; perhaps he didn't know himself. He started phoning me afterwards; his conversation was light but laced with innuendo. Unlike other people I didn't find him attractive. He was stocky and short, too short, and though his eyes were azure blue, a unique colour, he had an unusually wide mouth. Once he kissed me on the cheek and it was as if a slippery, stretched rubber-band had been pressed against my face. Yet his flirting was harmless. I liked the way he was never angry or offended when I spurned his advances. I think he probably liked the challenge. Finally he won out. One night at his place, I was depressed and tired, and he started touching me and my body responded and I thought, well, maybe this is inevitable, perhaps he can teach me something; I was so conscious of the effects of my religious upbringing and so afraid of being a prude. So I made myself do it. The fact that I'd only ever viewed him as a platonic friend made the sex seem incestuous and embarrassing. I had to forget who he was and concentrate on his any-man's body.

Afterwards I feared he wouldn't phone me again as he'd finally gotten what he'd wanted. But he did call, just never talked of sex again and I thought, well, I guess it was good we got that out of the way.

When I search my mind for the physical details of that night, I only find the occasional flash of a limb in darkness, the crucial whereabouts of sperm, blood and saliva are lost. Am I right to be so concerned about my body in light of the loss of Claude's?

The day after the Paris vacation he was hospitalized, yet I was still engulfed in naivety, assumed he'd be released a few days later. When I spoke with Claude on the phone, he said, 'I really enjoyed the trip. If you go on another one, I'd like to go again.'

Did illness seem unreal to me because I'd been too unaware of the body in general? Am I not sensual enough?

The evening of the Arc de Triomphe fiasco was Claude's last as an active man. The next day he became sick and couldn't leave his bed. What did we do for his last night out? I fulfilled his biggest request, made his greatest dream come true.

'I took him to a bathhouse,' I said to Bill weeks later. 'When he was sick, dying and full of the virus, I took him to a bathhouse so he could have unsafe sex and infect half of Europe.'

Claude so wanted to go to a gay sauna. 'Theirs are probably different from ours.' He said he wanted to have sex with a Frenchman, thought it'd be different than with a Canadian.

'All right,' I said. I looked up 'Sauna' in the *Gay Guide*, found an address and checked it on my *Carte de Paris*. There was a bathhouse not far from where we were staying. You only had to take two streets to get there, so he could find his way back to the hotel himself. I wouldn't go inside but would accompany him there, let him have his fun. I was looking forward to having him out of my hair for the evening.

Claude napped until 9 p.m. We both headed out onto the quiet, shadow-striped street for what was to be Claude's last night on the town. His face looked drawn and he limped slowly from one foot to the other.

A block from the sauna we entered a café, sat at a table. Claude carefully ate half of a ham baguette; he'd hardly eaten all day. He drank two coffees and the caffeine had a stimulating effect as he livened up considerably. 'I can't wait to see what it's like in their saunas,' he said.

'You can give me all the gory details tomorrow.'

Claude's breathing was laboured. He seemed to have some kind of phlegm in his throat and went to the washroom to cough it up. We sat quietly for half an hour. Then when he tried to stand, he couldn't get up. I helped him to his feet. He swayed a little.

'Are you sure you want to go?' I said.

'Oh, I'm fine.' On the street he came alive, walking with great strides and laughing. Then we stood in front of the sauna.

'OK, Claude. You remember how to get home. Go to those traffic lights, turn right and walk five blocks and you'll come to our hotel area.'

'I know it.'

'It probably costs less than thirty francs. Give them one of the blue bills.'

'See you tomorrow,' Claude said. 'And thanks.' He winked at me. He turned towards the main entrance.

Claude stepped forward, approached, entered; the door closed behind him. I stood staring for a minute at the dark, shut door. The light above flashed, *Sauna pour Hommes 18+*. I walked away. I wanted to see what Napoleon's Tomb looked like lit-up.

... staring into the casserole, vegetables, sauce, meat spinning over and under each other, round and round ...

The next day Claude told me, 'They have small rooms and you just have sex with whoever you want. I did three guys at one time. Was it ever fun. They liked my accent. This one old guy kept following me until I told him to beat it. Then there was a larger room and all these really nice guys in it.'

... corn tumbled over beans over carrots over broccoli ... Suddenly I said it, 'That guy you drove to the airport. He died last week.'

Both my parents stopped chewing.

I said the truth. 'There was finally some cancerous thing in his brain, caused by AIDS. He died of HIV-related illness. Nobody knew he was sick.'

My parents put down their forks and stared.

I lifted the spoon from the plate, shovelled a heap of steaming, dripping casserole into my mouth.

I will never go back to Paris.

Claude lay in bed the last three days as I freely wandered the streets of the Left Bank, visited the ornate cemetery in Montparnasse, lingered by my favourite fountain at St. Michel where a brooding, bearded Poseidon watches from a wall of seashells that clatter and tremble as water roars around them.

What was Claude thinking about as he lay staring at the grey walls, the cracked mirror? Did he realize what was happening to him? Each evening I returned to the hotel with some fruit and a baguette that Claude tried to eat. We talked about going to a hospital but I assumed he just had the flu and Claude said I was probably right. He told me he did have ulcers and this might be them acting up again.

On the plane home Claude was relaxed. As expected he'd forgotten our quarrels, our petty disagreements. He never accumulated resentment. I think now that's why there were so many mourners at his funeral. He clung to people regardless of what they did. You could speak insensitively, not return his calls, stand him up at the cinema, even leave him dying in some dingy Paris hotel room and the next week he'd phone you up and say, 'That was fun; let's do it again.' I said goodbye to Claude at Spadina subway station. He said, 'Thanks for the trip,' and got on the escalator.

Two months later when Bill phoned me and said Claude had died, it was as if someone had slapped me in the face with a steel-buckled belt, then slapped me again, then slapped me again.

I have no photos of Claude at all. I did not take pictures and have nothing concrete to remind me of him. I wanted to ask for the photo I took in front of Notre Dame, but after his death there was a huge fight between his family and his two lovers (yes, two lovers, I didn't even know he had one) as everyone wanted his very expensive possessions. So I didn't bother getting involved.

It is his silence that I cannot accept.

Claude, you could've told me. I would've understood.

Or would I? Perhaps all illness is attended by feelings of weakness and weakness engenders shame and the shame is worse for people with AIDS because there are all those pundits shaking their fingers on TV screens and trying to close borders. Perhaps he saw the world as contaminated by the need to judge; everyone, even close friends were sick with the disease. I'd thought difficulties were magnified by silence but maybe speaking makes them more real. And it's clear now that Claude did not want that. He experienced much change in his short life – transforming himself from Timiskaming streetperson to small-town father to gay, urban bar boy – but the change announced to him by a callous clinic doctor could not be incorporated into his life without upsetting everything else. So he simply chose not to believe it. That was the secret to his seamlessly perfect act. And surely that was why he liked to have me as a friend, because of my stupidity, my towering, colossal blindness to the flesh, which may have seemed to him like optimism, even faith, something he fed off and felt sustained by.

Claude denied his disease in the same way that people go to Paris.

So if I say Claude tried to believe HIV was a fantasy, does that excuse him? Can I remove him from the moral grid and place him in a space beyond judgment, or does that mean blindness and an attempt to live on the Champs-Elysées forever?

On our last morning in France, Claude was feeling better. Perhaps the promise of a return home energized him.

Together we went to the Eiffel Tower. I'd already been and Claude had no interest in going up it as that was expensive; so we relaxed on a bench at its base beside the famous row of fountains. I like to remember us at that moment. We weren't arguing and for once our differing desires complemented each other, Claude happily anticipating his return to a familiar place, as I brimmed full of a satisfaction gleaned from a brief yet thrilling immersion in an other world. We both gazed ahead into the arching streams of sputtering water as above rose the quintessential symbol of Paris. The steel support rods and latticed cross-beams joined seamlessly together over our heads, as the gleaming, silver tower rose with peaceful grace into the empty, blue sky.

A Piano Shudders

To Tom, the Royal Conservatory of Music looms like a castle, a battleship, a mortuary, a cathedral.

But the new teacher he's chosen is Mrs Cho. At the sound of her name, his chest fills with air and he floats up into the sky. Mrs Cho's face is a spheriform moon perpetually smiling, and when she laughs, light dances across her glasses, abruptly flits away when she pivots her head. Her hair's a labyrinth of twisting curls that bend like the stalks of plants in a jungle, and her suit fabric (usually cherry or vermilion) climbs wave-like over her bosom and subsides into the swirling eddy-like pleats of her skirt. Her studio is spartan, no rug, photos or distractions, just the grand piano standing in the centre like a lung.

Tom views only what's before her outstretched finger targeting piano keys, his knuckles, notes on the page.

'My, you're a quick learner,' she says.

She never asks about his former teachers, those ancient ladies blooming mould in suburban, death-shuttered bungalows. He senses he now has no past. He is sixteen years old. This is the start of his life.

His mother has become thoroughly distraught. 'And now he's going to an Oriental,' she sniffs. 'Some foreigner we've never met or even heard of when he could be seeing Mabel. Mabel, head of the Ladies' Auxiliary. Mabel, teacher at the School for the Especially Talented. Mabel, born to study, play and teach piano, whose fingers are long and rectangular as piano keys. Mabel, my own dear personal friend. I should never have given him a cheque but he's gotten so pigheaded, and I was sure he'd soon hate that crazy Chink, right, Arthur?'

'Sure,' her husband says, pressing the channel remote.

First lesson Mrs Cho tells Tom not to dig his digits into the keyboard, clutching at its cliff-edge. 'If you're afraid to fall, then fall.'

Next she demands he slice off his forearm muscles and hurl them out the window. 'Put your hands on the keys and lean into the piano, a tight muscle is a bloodclot between you and the instrument, you must flow to it, it flows to you, you and it are one and the same, I christen thee, Steinway.'

She tells him to detach his eyeballs. 'Forget the page and let your eyes drop, watch your fingers dance across the black/white right/wrong of the world and hear the harmony it all makes.'

Finally she says to balance on the piano bench, one foot lifted in air, as his eyes fixate on the dust mote on the ceiling bulb. 'Yes, there are rules to be followed. But remember: phrases grow and die of their own accord. Strike and don't strike, listen and don't listen.'

When he crouches and rams his fingers into the keys, they swallow him. The piano ignites, erupts, up through the loop of fire he flies, a missile; his head strikes – breaks through the ceiling to disrupt a fourth-storey violin class. Tom spits out plaster fragments while an old man brays, 'You young scallywag!' He tastes acrid carpet dust on his tongue as he squints down at Cho's beaming face. 'That was good,' she says, 'except your third finger stumbled on the B-flat.'

Next they select his program. 'One major work from each of the five musical periods plus a concert étude.'

She ushers him through the Conservatory's library, its walls battalioned with leukous, peeling manuscripts. They scrutinize the hell-black eighth-notes hurtling along Beethoven's staff lines, the prissy-savage elegance of Mozart's claw-curved phrases, the devil's intervals trapped in Chopin's chromatic mazes, then the whole system exploding into the falling pipe shards and thumbtacks of the twentieth century. They forage, ransack, pilfer.

The result: Bach, Italian Concerto; Beethoven, Sonata Op. 31 No. 2; Chopin, *Fantasie-Impromptu*; Debussy, *La Cathédrale Engloutie*; Coulthard, Étude No. 2.

'An intelligent program,' says Mrs Cho. 'The examiner will be impressed.'

Tom auditions for a concert, performs the Third Movement of

Beethoven's Tempest Sonata and reaps an A.

Mother says, 'With Mabel you'd get A plus.'

Mother fidgets, gapes at Father on the chesterfield. Her eyes plead as she cries, 'Cousin Fred is not well … I can't find the right sofa covers … Do you want me to put more cheese in your lunch?' Father stares blankly at the TV screen. Mother's head soon drops, an abandoned marionette's, her body deflating. But when the door slams and there's Tom, her face radiates as she rushes to the door. 'What do you want for supper?'

On Saturday she seats him at the kitchen table and says, 'I don't know. Is this the best way? To get into university, you'll need a good grade on your exam. Why did you choose the downtown conservatory, it's so far away, two hours from here! And you practise all the time there – oh so they've got these big grand pianos, well, ours is the one you grew up on, *mister*, and you may think you're so high and mighty, special, gifted and talented, but that little upright's done everything for you.' Her mouth droops. 'Billy and Tim, all the neighbourhood boys miss you and wonder why you're not here.'

The subway train rocks, lurches, his knee pounds a pole, gassmell intensifies, wheels whinny and screech, the metallic clicking accelerates to a shattering pitch, he's on a rocket bulleting skyward, BAM he strikes the sun – euphoria.

Mother is to meet Mrs Cho. Tom's hands flutter outside his pant pockets as he shuffles along, face lowered. Mother's head's perched upright, the click of her shoes on tile as even as a metronome. Tom finds himself beholding things through his mother's eyes: the archways with their fatuous loops and curlicues, the hanging portraits of lizard-faced professors too haughty to smile. At the hall's end, a petite, smirking totem: Mrs Cho. They stop. Tom inhales, wipes his lips, ahems. His mouth, sandpaper. 'Mother, this is Mrs Cho – Mrs Cho, my mother.'

Then Mrs Cho opens her lips but it is not her voice that emerges.

Tom glares, bug-eyed, as she disintegrates before him. '*Good you got come here. Nice for me meet you. Tom ven good studen.*'

69

When they say goodbye, Mother turns, lips pursed as if tasting sewer water, and then a sharp metallic glint in one cornea, bright, knowing, and triumphant.

But in the studio Mrs Cho speaks and Tom's sail inflates, her words are hordes of hornets that encircle, lift him up, up, up, he plunges into the piano, blood blazing, his brain, lava, insane with the scent of lemon-wax – hammers crash and wallop, dampers pummel, life pounds through his bloodstream and as he nears Beethoven's fire-blasting summit, he lets out an exultant cry that shakes the conservatory walls. Mother is exiting through the foyer and a flake of plaster hits her nose. 'Place isn't even built properly,' she says.

The next seven months, Tom practises eight hours a day, twelve hours on weekends, scribbles schoolwork at midnight. The pieces must be chiselled into his fingertips, branded on his brain. He collapses into bed, exhausted. In his dreams piano keys flap like loose teeth.

Examination day is May 20 and its approach is the slow ascent on a rollercoaster. The seat-back gouges Tom's vertebrae, the sun spears his retinas, the rackety grinding of multitudinous wheels beneath his feet, at the peak there will be silence, then – the fall.

As he approaches the apex, the cries of 'Mabel, Mabel' crescendo and at last he says, 'All right, already.'

Next week, a clean seven days prior to his exam, he'll visit Mabel.

Mother's ebullient. 'She'll invite some friends. It'll be a real recital, and she'll give a critique that's perceptive and helpful.'

Cho's interpretations are safely rooted to all his internal organs.

The day is sultry, the sun cocked behind their heads. From the car, houses pass like gingerbread cutouts.

They halt at a dwarfish, stucco bungalow, venetians drawn. The dun carpet slobbers down the front porch like a tongue.

Mother says, 'We're finally here.'

On the threshold, facial features. Chocolate-chip eyes, strawberry freckles, hoary hair in pigtails. Irma, Mabel's housemate.

Hitherto, she'd been Tom's Sunday school teacher.

She's unbarred the door and one hand snaps back and forth like a fish snatched from water. 'Come, come, everyone's waiting.'

The corridor smells like mints, the walls freckled with photos of Mabel. She stands fondling flowers or shaking gloves with conductors. In some she performs, her torso ramrod straight or curled over the keyboard like a comma.

Tom detects a murmuring and the squeaking of chair legs. He steps into a chamber jammed full of elderly ladies seated, holding teacups. In the centre, lofty, soundless, stone still, Mabel. The whispering dissipates as her head rotates mechanically toward him. Her eyes lock with his, then wander over the full length of his body, stare back into his face, one hand sensually caressing a stiff tulip stem.

He steps forward, 'How do you do,' and proffers his hand. Her rigid fingers fold around his. Rectangular shafts of ashen hair drop like pillars on each side of her horse face.

Then the corners of her mouth collapse, her gaze solidifies, pupils shrink to rifle-barrels. An explosive exhalation. Abruptly she sits. 'So what will you play for us?' Her dress is cut square as a box.

'My whole program if you don't mind. It lasts about one hour.'

'Good.' She nods her head. 'There's the piano. You may commence when ready.'

Irma sings out, 'Wait just a minute. I have to go to the bathroom!'

Mabel's eyes glaze over. Her head turns and she snaps, 'Irma, must you do that now!'

'I need some water or I'll cough all the way through.'

Mabel's nostrils flare.

'Maybe he should get used to that,' says a turbaned woman. 'He'll have to when he's a concert pianist.'

Ladies purr agreement.

'Ah yes.' Mabel shifts in her seat. 'Coughs, paper rustling, even people tapping pencils all come to harass the already overwrought nerves of the concert performer.' She halts. '*I* know.' Her stare bores into Tom's head. 'Once I was at a concert by Anton Kuerti where he was playing Mozart's Sonata No. 5.' Her eyelashes quiver and Tom is enticed into the space between her words. What goes on in her head? He peers into an ebony chasm, half-terrified he'll tumble forward. 'During the third movement, Anton stopped and said, "Could the woman who keeps coughing please leave now." No one got up. So Anton's wife hollered, "He said NOW!"'

Laughter ripples round the room. Mabel's smile forms, congeals and she hisses, 'The woman had to leave.'

Irma reappears, stepping over people and saying sorry, and before Tom knows it, the piano is before him, keys glinting like daggers in a tray as he inhales a mothball perfume. In his cranium he performs the first bars of the Italian Concerto. Is he ready? Yes. Begin. His right index finger depresses F, his left hand creates a chord.

But the keys are rocks that barely budge and he must pound with clenched muscles, then tilt forward, propelling his body weight into the keyboard. Perspiration drops crawl down his scalp, as somewhere a vacuum sucks the harmonies away. All his notes sound identical, his phrases formless. His music's an aged man muttering in monotone.

Between pieces, the ladies applaud while Mabel scowls smugly. Tom plays on, feels he's wading through tar, lost in a dream, a musical purgatory. He batters at the keyboard, thwacks the pedal to the earth, tries to wake the beast from its slumber, but the piano shudders. When Tom plays the final bar, it dies.

The fervent clapping of hands.

The ladies chatter. 'Just beautiful ... Oh, he's so talented ...'

Mabel surveys him as if he's a mountain-face she's about to scale. 'You are talented,' she blurts. 'I don't say that to everyone.' She sips her tea. 'But I can't help saying, your Beethoven, *The Tempest*, is a tempest in a soup bowl, not the real tempest.'

The room goes silent.

As Tom swivels round, the piano bench chirps. 'What do you mean?'

'Where's the guts, the fury, the storm in that piece? I couldn't hear it at all.' Her voice is loud, yet she eyes him cautiously. 'I'm reminded of Arthur Schnabel. Now he,' she says, 'was a teacher!' Her eyes spark. 'He said '*The Tempest* is chaos and tragedy in 3/8 time. It demands a heroic sound on the largest scale. Tom, your mezzo-forte is too soft. Your fortissimo should just take the ceiling off the room. Not just with the Beethoven but in all your pieces, the tone level is too low –'

'I found this piano hard to control.'

'– in my day, when I was a girl studying, no, not studying, sacrificing my life for Arthur Schnabel –' He feels he's being pelted with pebbles and melts with nostalgia for she's his past: direct, brutal, unassailable, not smeared with Cho's vagueness. 'He would shake me, slap me, almost throw me to the ground and say, "Mabel, where is that sound?! I want to hear it, feel it, be assaulted by it. Give, Mabel," he'd scream. "Give! Give! Give!"'

Jaw clenched, Tom makes a fist and strikes the keyboard. 'Like that?'

With his first question, Mabel's face illuminates. She springs up, pushes her way through the two tall women in front, one of whom tumbles to the carpet.

Irma says, 'Everyone, we have cake and cookies downstairs,' and as the room empties, Tom's mother calls back, 'Mabel likes giving lessons.'

Mabel talks rapidly, demands he commence from the beginning, stops him every few bars, makes him repeat, more tumultuous here, more sedate there, faster, slower, staccato, more pedal. Half experimenting, Tom slips complacently into his old passive role. Mabel sabotages his repertoire, horks all over his Chopin, calls his Bach bland and bloodless, says his Debussy is an empty box, and as for his twentieth-century Coulthard, 'Nancy-pantsy. My grandmother could play better.'

Her cheeks scintillate as he battles through Beethoven, not flowing but fighting with the music. Mabel clucks approval, beats her hands together when he must accelerate.

Yet everything feels different:

- The music's shapes are now easier to see.
- The sounds only take place outside him.
- He sees the music has existed long before his birth. Also he has never written music.
- Now he does not feel anything except the slight fear of screwing up.
- He understands that musicians are assembly-line products, canned sardines with notes on the packaging.

Suddenly it's like the days before Cho when piano pieces had nothing to do with you but were minefields to scuttle through while applauded by halls stuffed with sartorially overwrought observers, their ears cocked, judging. He perceives Mabel beside him helping control this monstrosity that could pounce, sinking its teeth into his jugular.

Her face shines, hands uplifted, beige circles in her armpits. 'Yes,' she exclaims as he charges up the crescendo peak, 'you have it, yes,' and she lets out a boisterous cry, the ecstatic shout made when you reach the mountaintop to see no other summits soar higher.

When finished, Tom huddles, breathing heavily; his brain whirls. They'd only explored two pieces in detail. What about the others?

Mabel sits happily, her lips arched. 'Oh Tom,' she chuckles. 'I've gotten you all in a snit.' Irma's drumbeat footsteps up the staircase as Mabel whoops, 'He's upset!' yet says, 'But there's a solution. Play the new style daily and your fingers will get used to the technique.' What follows is an intoxicating silence as Tom feels himself invisibly drawn forward. Then Mabel stands, leviathan, a resolute, sabre-solid figure against a murky horizon. 'Come here again next week and I'll listen for the improvement.'

Irma escorts them out, says, 'Bye-bye,' jerks back her head and shuts the door like a jack-in-the-box closing its lid.

At night Tom's bed is a spindly raft reeling on wave-whipped seas, his body gyrates, thrashes while empty horizons gape all round and demons hiss in his ear, 'You'll fail the exam, not get to university and never want to play again.' All day images slice his brain like razors and he shrieks 'No!' at the songless future as Mabel's face simpers like a gargoyle, Mrs Cho's smile suffocates him with guilt, witches' claws clutch at his organs and pull in a thousand directions at once. Each day is a death knell: Monday, Tuesday, Wednesday, Thursday ...

He quivers on the piano bench, his hands hovering over keys that resemble piranhas. Condemnatory eyes sear the nape of his neck. Who is right?

Mother watches him, her mouth an O.

One day she goes shopping.

Pallid-faced, Tom enters the living room where the ground lurches and pitches like the floorboards of a ship.

'Dad, I have a question.'

Father turns, TV light fondling his cheek. He is maroon, then turquoise.

'Who is right, the young teacher I pay money to, or mother's old friend, Mabel? I need to know.'

Father glowers across the coffee table that seems as immense, level and empty as an Arctic ice shelf. His forehead pleats. 'Music teachers?' Question marks fill his eyes.

Tom thinks, You can help me, Dad, speak!

Father turns, pokes the channel remote. 'Who's better-lookin'?'

'I guess, Mrs Cho.'

'Well, take her.' Tom stares at his father's ear, circular and beige like a rubber sink-plug. '*Bowling for Dollars* must be here somewhere.'

The TV set instantaneously blankens to a thousand, palpitating, salt-and-pepper speckles; an incessant SHHH.

Tom skulks back to his room.

But at night he remembers the void screen, recollects his first day in the Royal Conservatory's registrar's, his heart banging against his rib cage, as sixteenth-notes flew in joyful chaos across the empty screen in his mind. As he relives it all, his body levitates. Is this what happiness is? He opens his eyes, falls back onto the soft mattress. All

75

around him, pitch darkness. His room's full of secrets.

On exam day the world goes mute.

The steady ringing of silence envelops Tom as he boards the bus, subway, escalators, then crouches outside the concert hall.

When it's his turn, he wanders onto the stage, regards the audience area, a black hole, an examiner concealed in shadows. A male bass voice. 'Please begin once you're seated.'

Tom sits. Keys phosphoresce beneath the spotlight and the piano lid slants skyward.

He closes his eyes, wants to weep but stares at the triangle of empty space beneath the piano lid, calms himself.

He begins to play Bach. Nervously. The first line, second line, first page, soon he's halfway. Then somewhere in the Development, he glimpses Mrs Cho and Mabel standing on opposite sides of the piano. Mrs Cho grins, Mabel scowls. Tom gasps, is instantly held locked in the terrible tension of two magnetic forces pulling in opposite directions and in one second his body will tear in half, his intestines falling into a messy heap on the piano bench.

'Go away!' he cries, then suddenly, 'You're both useless;' and as he gapes at the blank space between them, something in him clicks, and the women transmogrify into two sky-high precipices as a salt-water wave rushes across the stage and he's lifted up, pulled forward. Wind ruffles his hair, the piano lid forms a sail and he flows between the cliffs out to the great glimmering sea beyond. Water-drops splash his face, salt-seaweed smells suffuse his nostrils while gulls cry faintly like crystal clinking.

His heartbeat is the ebb-tide wafting him; as his breath flows out and in, so his fingers step freely from white key to black, wander effortlessly over the keyboard's unthreatening topography.

Teachers' words have dissolved to dust-specks and his own untrammelled feelings rise, collect, dissipate, rise, collect ... on and on.

Is there still somewhere a monstrous claw ready to clutch him?

Out of the corner of his eye he perceives a tree-lined shore so far,

far away; he's unequivocally, invincibly, superbly alone.

Playing the final chord is simple as dropping a stone into water. Enveloped in a plastic membrane he's afraid will break, he turns, regards the black sloping wall of audience-seats, the examiner a lone star in a night sky.

The bespectacled man sits, beaming, fingers on tear-drenched face, as his pencilled hand leaps along the comment sheet. Tom feels breathless, flushed, exhausted. From his bench, the examiner seems brazenly unimportant, his words lost insects spinning in the air.

So unlike pianos, their sheer, unchanging, weighted, stable, rooted, unconquerable solidity; Tom realizes they've been unjudgingly alongside him for years now. Before commencing the second piece, he leans forward and gently kisses the piano on its nameplate.

Capturing Varanasi

'The bodies are burned in a roaring fire that restores, heals and liberates.' My voice trembles as I say the words I've written. I hate reading out loud but if I refuse, Guy will grab my notes and recite in a mocking tone that's infuriating. I wonder if he's like this with other women. 'Flames like lapping tongues of snakes flicker round the body's outer edges, crack through the shell-hard skin of ego, penetrate the inner recesses and obliterate everything.' Guy glares statue-still, sweat drops congealing in rows above his eyebrows. 'Consumed are muscles stretched and torn through years of toil, sinews taut with longing and unrequited desire, the intestines twisted into knots of anxiety and unending grief, the hollow husk of the heart. As the body blackens, the soul withdraws its tentacles from the body' – Guy turns away, starts picking his fingernails – 'and is transformed from earth-bound and sullied' – my voice quavers, this is why I've come here, isn't it? – 'to a state of pure, untarnished bliss, the essence that gave birth to the world but is not of the world. The exact moment of that ecstatic release and transformation is not known. Spectators can only pray silently as the ashes drift skyward, eventually vanishing into the crystalline, sun-drenched light of the glorious Heavens.'

Guy grabs, pulls me to the bed, presses his saliva-hot mouth against mine and I'm driven down into the inescapable realness of my body, where my pulse throbs in my eardrums, and a billion skin pores are mouths that open and shriek to be touched. His sweat cedar-sweet on me, I want to taste it, drink, bathe, would swim in an ocean of it.

I scream at myself: Forget this loser! You hardly know him – but my arms snake round his plank-hard back, press him closer.

He growls, 'You fucking know how to tell a story, Cheryl.'

Sitting back I see his quadrangle jaw, large pupils, pale and luminous as ghosts' eyes.

Through the window the rising, ululating, nasal whine of Hindi pop music, wail of street vendors, chaotic chorus of a million chiming bicycle bells. Our day's beginning.

'Or perhaps you're lying,' he says, smirking. 'You say half the time you talk about people, it's not true.' He hasn't understood what I meant. 'It's such a load of B.S.' and he reaches, again my face in his neck; below, a constellation of freckles stretching across his beauti- fully arching chest, my hands press biceps, twitching rocks beneath loose sticky skin. My ear on his rib cage, I can't hear his heart yet he's more alive than any abstractions I conjure up, but when he hisses in my ear, 'If Ms Betty could see us now,' it's like he's thrown ice-water in my face.

He thinks we're defying our boss, as if she hadn't expected or even cared we'd like each other. As his unshaven chin skids along my forearm, I remember Betty's eyebrows arching. 'I'm surprised you want to go overseas. You're supposed to be the housebound one.'

'I just have to get out of this city,' I'd said.

She realized Trevor had left me. There was a tactful silence. She put a file into the drawer and closed it. When she later said that Guy would be travelling with me, I was indifferent and sure I'd remain so, though the past year he'd been hovering around the edges of my life and, when visiting Toronto, always made eye contact with me at meetings; when shaking hands would hold mine a second too long.

As I get up, a click, flash, I turn. Guy is clutching his camera.

'Guy, I actually don't like having my photo taken without being warned. I broke up with someone who took my photo all the time.'

'Sorry.'

He puts down his camera, pondering. An old boyfriend. Is he putting away this significant bit of information or thinking about what film to use today?

I realize that I hope he's thinking both.

I gather my paper, pens, tape recorder, put them into my sack. 'Today we're visiting the west side of the city,' I say, businesslike. 'Three temples, two mosques and a huge bazaar.' On my skin still his cedar scent. Through the window a minaret like an arrow pointed at the sky, yet it's not solid but shimmers as if beneath water, changing. Good. I want everything to be unstable.

Soon Guy's fully dressed in his striped pants and vest and a white cotton T-shirt with a black shoelace tied round his neck, hair gathered in a ponytail; his white cheek skin's so vulnerably white, exposed and far too fair for the harsh Indian sun. He gazes doe-eyed, breathing quietly through his full, moist lips parted just slightly and all at once I want to grab, hurl him to the floor, tear away everything that hides him from me.

Fool! I scream. He's practically a stranger, the trip's only five days, this isn't why you're here! I grind the words into my brain like forcing glass shards under my skin.

Guy says huskily, 'I'd like to photograph the burning bodies. Get their final moment. That'd be cool,' and something whiplashes in my skull.

In Canada I uprooted my life. I had no choice.

One day Trevor simply said, 'This isn't working. I have no more feelings for you. It's best we move on,' and that was that. I stood holding a steaming plate I'd removed from the dishwasher. A few days later the moving truck came and then all his furniture was gone. Inexplicably after ten years. 'There's no one else, Cheryl; nothing wrong with you; it's just time,' and he shrugged his shoulders. I'd thought he was as predictable as the buses that passed our condo every ten minutes, his alarm clock that rang 6:47 each morning, the click of his key in the lock at 5:50 and his yearly vacation beginning July 1 and ending July 21. Surely he'd been changing but I was blind thinking once a pattern is established and the wheels of habit set in motion, inertia makes it impossible to escape, even if you want to. I'd once edited an article on Hinduism for Betty and read, 'their acceptance of the temporariness of all conditions, the shifting ungrounded kaleidoscope of human expectation;' I'd thought, how horrible, how could anyone live like that?

Yet after six months in a near-empty apartment, I stood in the huge, cavernous Pearson Airport and looked out at the desolate runway stretching on across flat empty fields towards the blank horizon;

there were no images in my brain, only a steady drumbeat at the very base of me, pure, relentless and connected to nothing specific outside of it: I want, I want, I want …

Guy and I enter the stream of life. Horn-blaring taxis hurtle past sari'd women leading goats between whirring cycle-rickshaws whose spinning wheels flash in the sun; barefoot vendors drag wood past wagons full of bulging sacks as we step between cow paddies, traverse crumbling sidewalks, pass through clouds of bus exhaust, incense, everywhere the smell of excrement and sweet basmati rice, a chaotic jumble of storefronts below ramshackle signs, 'Thumbs Up Best Tastie Drinking.' Barbers shave customers on street corners as teenage boys splash ochre paint on walls, while a Western-suited businessman spits in the gutter and straightens his tie; a dragon-faced woman clutches Guy's trousers and holds. Every minute a different smiling man approaches, offers tea. 'Would you like to see carpet shop' or gift emporium or curry saleshouse or astrology room. 'Ma'am, I see your mind is a butterfly, it cannot settle.' Cows saunter like bored tourists, chew cud in intersections, whip their tails at flies leapfrogging about their haunches. Everywhere white-washed temples stand like gleaming wedding cakes.

'The city and everything in it,' I will write, 'is a metaphor for something else.' That means that Guy and I are metaphors too. But for what? Guy points at distant columns of smoke twirling voluptuously in the sky, winks at me and I swear silently.

Into the narrow alleyway of the Old City, round a corner, on the wall, a painting of Shiva, his black-ringed eyes, garish scarlet lips. I stare, close my eyes, immediately feel I've left my body. I swoop up over the city and am watching from a god's perspective. I now see myself with complete objectivity, and in truth I am absurd. All of life roaring round me, yet my mind burrows into a dark hole. I recognize the telltale signs: the hand unsteady as I touch a railing, eyes darting to Guy, then away, then back, the shallow breathing, and the sudden inhalation as Guy turns, touches my arm.

Foolish and amazing. I thought I was beyond all this, but here it is blooming as if I were fifteen and life had never sunk its claws into my skin.

Guy says, 'That's a pretty big Krishna,' pronouncing it French-style: 'Kreechna.' He has problems with English names.

'Sir, it's actually Rama.'

'Rama-Krishna-Hinda, they're all wild statues, that's all I know.'

When a humpbacked beggar approaches holding a tin can in three fingers, Guy flicks in a rupee coin, says, 'Don't spend it on booze, eh,' and laughs.

With horror I realize his careless insensitivities attract me. He is self-enclosed, a stone; nothing comes in and nothing goes out. Solid. I can throw myself against him, disintegrate into spume, fog, smoke.

The laneway widens and now we're in a teeming crowd, rows of stalls piled with hills of violet, ochre, puce powders, beads, jewels, stacked statuettes. I turn immediately and see Guy is gone. A curtain falls around me. So this is how it would feel to be here alone. What's happened to my heartbeat? Yes, there it is. Am I returning to my original shapelessness, youth's form before sex and desire put streaks in the smooth wood of my skull? I take a deep breath, watch turbaned men arguing over a donkey and just feel lost. A tank-grey cow passes, the wiry hair on its ribbed stomach brushing my T-shirt. Finally I see Guy's face, a buoy bobbing on a wild sea of heads, now transformed into a wrinkled gargoyle of grief as his shrunken eyes dart. A hot liquid shoots through my limbs, my lungs inflate and I feel I'm rising to the sky, will merge with the sun.

I force myself back down into my body.

'Guy!'

He looks towards me, the lined mask vanishes and his baby-face beams. He comes, embraces me just for a second. He speaks softly. 'So tell me about this bazaar. I'd like to know about it.'

I explain that the Golghur Market was founded in the Middle Ages and little has changed since that time. Guy listens, head down, quiet as a child.

At lunch I wrap words around the food.

'These are pureed chick peas; they mash them up and fry them in ghee; this ochre paste is best with oil and ...' Sentences make designs in the air; they can coat the lining of his stomach, protect his body from evil.

He abruptly spits into a serviette. 'Oh, it's awful,' he says.

When he's finished drinking his mango lassi, Guy becomes very quiet.

Then he looks up at me and says, 'Whenever I'm away from Montreal, I don't think of it at all, you know. I think of Chibougamau instead. It's the place I was born. That's funny, eh? You'd expect I'd think of Montreal 'cause I see it every day, but I don't really like it. It's so busy and noisy. Not as much as here ... but it's the same kind of place.' Guy looks at me searchingly. 'My mother and brother still live in Chibougamau and I think it's a good town. Friendly people, everybody talks together; we have black flies there the size of your head. One look at you and they'd gobble you up in a mouthful.' He puts a finger on his plate, runs it through a puddle of sauce. 'I'd like to go back and I will some day. Maybe when I'm a old man and have saved money and don't have to do these magazine jobs. I can take pics of their tree stumps and bear turds arranged in pretty patterns. That place clears my head ... of all the confusing things in it.'

Later, changing money at the bank, he opens his passport and a second Guy emerges. I have to repress a laugh as I see his hair shorn, black-framed glasses, paisley tie pressed inside a too-tight button-down collar, travelling-salesman smile, but about his sad eyes something wavers, uncertain. A little boy in daddy's clothes.

He glances at me, snaps his passport shut.

We enter a museum.

'What's that say?' he asks.

'I can't read Hindi.'

'No?'

'I know. You think I know everything when I know diddly-squat.'

Guy laughs.

I enter a stone-walled washroom. The door bangs open and Guy barges in, closes the door, slides his nail-bitten fingers around my back, puts his tongue in my mouth and I gasp; he clutches round the small of my back and I wonder if this is only to cancel out the pasty Bay-Street-boy photo.

We are standing before the famous Golden Temple 'Whose bulbous dome,' I write, 'made from a ton of solid gold juts into the sky like a huge sliced onion.' In front, guards wearing black berets and toting machine guns prowl in a circle like caged lions.

We pass through the archway into a shadowy courtyard full of potted statues, a trickling, stone-hemmed stream. Beyond an inner archway, a dark room emitting the potent smell of incense, a sign 'Gentlemen not belonging to the Hindu faith are requested not to enter.' The inner sanctum off limits, its mystery protected. That satisfies me. I sit on a stone bench, take notes. A rake-thin yogi twists himself into pretzel shapes, and a wizened woman in beige widow's shawl pours perfumes, drops fistfuls of flowers over the lingam of squat Shiva. I write 'woman thanking God,' and hesitate. She has put her hands on her lips. Is she still thanking? I write, 'pondering God's greatness.' And next, 'thinking about lunch.' When you write something, by the time you finish the sentence, its meaning is no longer true. 'A yogi's face grimaced in pain' or is it disgust? ecstasy? 'Founded in 1620.' This is incontrovertible fact. I underline it.

I look up and in horror see Guy has started to take pictures. He holds the camera like a gun, aims at the kneeling woman. Click. The yogi locked in a photo frame. Click. The prostrate pilgrims ripped from their context and mounted like dead things on the wall.

In the widow's photo everything stops. Her flowers merely hover and will never touch her god's forehead. The yogi's legs will remain tangled an eternity, and the pilgrims' prayers will stop halfway to heaven.

The walls of our condo were covered with photographs of Trevor and me beside our boat, or helping each other build our cottage, or lounging on air mattresses in our swimming pool. People always take photos when the most heard sentence is 'It doesn't look like you at all.' Sometimes, talking to Trevor at the kitchen table, I couldn't tell whether the man before me or the picture on the wall behind him was more real.

Click. I have the sudden desire to grab and throw his camera against the wall. Still, Guy smiles at me. This is a job and I know the magazine needs photos. I sense Betty's presence, a benign deity in a Gap pantsuit who chants, 'The leaders of all great religions acted immorally some time or other.'

Later, on the bus, Guy says, 'I wish you'd told me what everything there was. I didn't know what to take pictures of and what to ignore. Can we see the burning bodies soon?'

I look into his beautiful pale eyes.

When the bus reaches the hill summit, I start to talk more about the religion here. 'Reincarnation is central. The Hindus believe it happens over and over. People die and after that, they're reborn, death, birth, on and on.'

Guy is chewing gum. I wonder where he found that here.

'Pretty freaky.'

'What do you mean?'

Surprisingly, he says something that's hard to answer. 'What's the point of all that repetition?'

I hesitate. 'Well, the transformations happen … just cause they happen.' I say. 'There is no point, I guess. But still the changing is important.' I get a new idea that pleases me. 'It's like marriage without children. It doesn't produce anything concrete that lasts. It just is what it is and you accept it has value.'

I begin to feel a bit depressed. Guy has lowered his head. He brushes a nail-bitten hand across his face.

On the other side of the aisle two long-limbed blond women in tie-dyed T-shirts are speaking German. One has an oval purple crystal she keeps rubbing on her forehead. New Age freaks.

Just for a second I imagine how I appear, a pasty white forty-one-year-old woman in designer jeans who talks smugly about reincarnation.

Late afternoon back at the hotel we make love on a bed criss-crossed with bands of sunlight. With Trevor I'd thought that the more we made love the more solid our relationship became, yet now I picture our earthbound bodies crashing inanely against each other. As Guy moves swiftly in and out of the bars of light, his appearance alters. Close up his cheeks are fat, Buddha-like, and his head turns and there's his sharp brow, sword-straight nose, a seigneur in a Renaissance painting; then he moans, his mouth like a dying fish, eyes flash, his nose wrinkles sarcastic, a snarling mongrel ... Can I catch him in my net? Would I know him if I saw him? I rejoice as I feel I never shall or could. Sunlight flickers on our moving skin and I imagine our bodies burning. After the conflagration we will shoot to the sky and only ashes will remain on the Earth.

At the room's wobbling desk I try to write about the Golden Temple. I wonder if I should use the widow's view, the yogi's view, what I imagine are their views or what seems my view or Guy's, backdropped by Betty's. Choosing one cancels out all the others.

Guy mutters in his sleep, French words issuing up from some childhood hearth in northern Quebec, a place I've never been. A world in his skull just tantalizingly beyond my reach.

At breakfast I study the hair curling over Guy's collar, and he talks on and on while cramming butter-dripping toast between his lips. My temples pulsate. Lifting my tea cup I see blue veins in my wrist. My desire for Guy is stronger today than yesterday. Does that make me more myself or less? Soon we're out on the sun-scorched streets, pushing through throngs that surge forwards, reverse flow, divide and spin in dizzying eddies. We cross oil-splattered dirt roads, dodge careening cycle-rickshaws, pass crying women clutching babies, a snake charmer on a traffic island, when the muezzin lets cry its plaintive prayer of longing. I stop, look up at the brutal cloudless sky. The ascending snakes of smoke are visible everywhere, seem titillatingly close. Guy gawks as if seeing a stripper reveal one knee. His camera swings from his neck like a cyclops eye.

Touching my pen in my pocket, I think, today for a short time, Guy, I'll research you. Waiting in the bus station, I talk about

Toronto and Montreal, ask Guy about his job, then say lightly, 'Do
you have a girl waiting for you there?'

His forehead creases. '*Une blonde*, you mean? Like, for a long
time?'

I shrug, pretending indifference.

'No. Last year I had someone. But not now.'

So he does have serious relationships.

In the corner stands an altar to Krishna, a blue-faced statuette,
flowers, glowing incense-stick. Before it a young man kneels, head
bowed.

Speaking carefree, 'What was she like?'

'She was short, slim.'

'I mean, her personality.'

'A fun girl.'

'Fun?' Am I fun? 'And?'

He eyes me. 'What?' He looks away. His limbs have become
stiff. 'She was fine.'

'Why'd you break up,' I say, yawning.

'It's ... It's kinda hard to describe. It's not fun.' His voice is
sharp.

I sit in silence. The praying man hasn't budged.

I hope Guy will ask about me but he says, 'I was at my brother's
wedding last year at this time and you know what happened there?
He was walking up the aisle to the front of the church and he realized
he forgot the ring. Can you imagine forgetting a thing like that? So
he whispered to me, "What do I do?" I was standing there; I had to
wear a tuxedo. In my pocket I had a pine cone – sometimes I carry
that with me because it was the pine cone of good luck.' Guy chuckles. I don't know if he's kidding me. 'Anyway I gave it to him and he
put it on top of her finger, like nobody would notice. She laughed
and everybody else there laughed but she was the loudest. Can you
imagine that?' He makes a huge smile; I can see his gums and the top
and bottom of every tooth. 'Being married by a pine cone! My
brother and Véronique did that and I wish them the best!'

After a minute I say, 'I was with a guy named Trevor. I think I

88

mentioned him to you. We didn't marry but were together a long time. Ten years actually.'

'Holy shit!'

I stare at him. 'I'm not sure I liked him.'

Do I even like you?

I turn away, imagine my body dissolving into sand particles that blow away in the wind.

Guy starts talking about the makes of tires on Indian trucks.

I hear the devotee muttering, '*Om ma mi mau svaahaa.*'

The whole bus lunges and rattles, and the seats shake beneath our butts as we try to see through windows smeared with swirling rivers of petrified mud.

We get off at the southern end of the city and approach the Durga Temple, an empty stone shell adorned with blurred carvings of gods and goddesses. The inside is an empty cavern full of boulders and heaps of rotting flowers. I can't help comparing it to the interior of a European cathedral and again realize that, despite my pretensions, I'm a Westerner, an outsider. I don't mind when Guy starts taking photos. The temple has been long dead, its days of transformation past.

But out the back entranceway, for the first time – I have to step back, not breathing – the Ganges River. Bits of light dance on the water flowing between cracked, parched banks and in the distance, pointy-roofed tents, rising pillars of smoke and, there, the glowing hissing fires that twist, turn and spark like flashing eyes, rooted stationary points that pierce through the dark swarming shapes having human forms.

'Jesus,' says Guy and I turn and see his mouth's open. Of course he doesn't look at the sky, only the fires. 'I hope it's not too far for my telephoto.'

I stand, words choked in my throat. 'Take my picture,' I say to distract him. 'I'll wade in the river.'

A grin forms in slow motion. 'That's a neat idea.'

I turn my back to him, keeping my face away.

I remove my sandals, hike up my pantlegs and step into the cold water that immediately stings my feet, as blood rushes to the surface of my skin. Against my soles the muddy bottom, neither solid nor soft. My body now looms large in my consciousness. It doesn't silence the voices in my head, but intensifies them. A fragment from a book: 'Though all manner of filth is thrown into the Ganges, Hindus bathe in it, believing the water washes away sin.' Modern people can't believe in sin. What are my sins? Tunnel vision. Idolatry. When the water's just above my knees, I stop, look up at the empty plain on the opposite shore, a straight line perfectly balanced. Suddenly, like machine-gun fire, click-click-click-click ... I hurl out one hand to shield myself and, bending at the waist, lose balance and fall sideways into the Ganges.

Every pore of my body jolts wide open as I'm surrounded by grey and floating particles of green. I don't know where is down or up but realize that beneath the surface he can't see me. Then my foot touches the earth and Guy, his camera, the temple, bounce back into view. My feet meld with the solid ground that ahead rises up into clay banks, like an extension of my own body that stretches on into the distant grey hills rising and falling as my breath-filled body expands and contracts.

Back on shore, Guy, 'God, Cheryl, I feel awful. I didn't mean to startle you. *Merde*, are your clothes wrecked?'

Dripping in a nearby teahouse, I suddenly say, 'Do you really have to take pictures at the burial ghats? I know Betty wants them but ... I'm amazed you haven't gone out there yourself yet; you know where it is.'

Guy says quietly, 'I like when you describe things to me. Otherwise it's not interesting.'

Then I say it and I'm surprised how easily the words come out. 'And Guy, are we gonna see each other when we get home or is this just one of your fuckfests you can tell Betty and your friends about?'

He tries to smile but his eyes water. My God, it's like watching a statue bleed. 'Actually, I thought ... we could see each other back home, maybe on weekends? We don't live that far apart.' Toronto and Montreal, the highway like a vein between them.

He puts his hand on the table, touches my thumb with his.

I say, 'OK.' I'm glad I only half-believe him.

Back on the bus, his leg against mine, somehow I feel I've experienced this before. In Hinduism, Shiva becomes Vishnu becomes mortal becomes a god … Trevor, Guy, others flash through my mind like a rapidly flipping deck of cards. The feeling I have is always the same but the outward form, the glistening eyes, hair-locks that buckle like waves in freak seastorms, a head sometimes ovular, discoid or quadrangle, always differs.

In the hotel I try to write words but my pen will only make lines that continue from one page to another.

That night in bed Guy has become solid. His face ossifies into a square-jawed warrior mask, as arms jut hard as a rock idol's and his birch legs reach deep into the earth. I clutch him as if clinging to a cliffside and look skyward.

The last day we rise with the sun and head out into the street.

The force of inevitability pushes us down past pens of stirring animals, through ghost-abandoned alleyways. Guy's demands are as real as metal bars pressed to the face. Our future has a shape now and I don't want it erased. We are going to the burning ghats. Fate has decided and it was all doomed to happen from the beginning. The moment the ghats were first mentioned, I knew my story would end there. Still, uncertainty hovers in the places the sun can't reach and about the edges of my vision there is a blurred tremoring.

Smoke billows up from the crackling fire reeking of balsam and sandalwood that stings my eyes, as here on this stone and mud platform, the last drama of life and death is carried out. We pass the No Cameras sign.

A glint-eyed man approaches, gesturing ferociously with his bony, paddle-shaped arms. His sparsely haired, domed head and beak-like nose give him the half-human, half-bird look of one of the Hindu eagle gods carved on temple entrances.

Guy lies, 'I know, no photos. I don't got any film anyway.'

Two *chandal*, Hindu outcasts, carry a bamboo stretcher with a body wrapped in multicoloured silk and adorned with gaudy flower wreaths and burning sticks of incense. Weeping relatives chant and sing as the beloved is carried to the river, submerged and after a brief priest's chanting brought and deftly lowered along the pyre. A billowing wall of flames as the logs snap and spit. Is this the precise moment when –

I hear a camera click.

Guy's now hidden like a sniper in a trench.

I step down but to the side, so people won't think I know him. The eagle man has turned away from us.

Before the burning fire, a statuette of Shiva. I close my eyes and, for the last time, leave my body, swoop up and view things from a god's height.

Again I appear ludicrous. I stand, clutching my desire for Guy like an old coin I found but refuse to throw away, while Guy opens and closes the doors of a cage that is at first small and then becomes bigger, inside which corpses writhe into nothingness.

Guy is no more substantial than a photograph, our two cities just dots on a paper map that when set on fire becomes ashes in five seconds. All of India is a cloak I've torn from the clasping hands of a greedy, gaunt-cheeked child, and wear wrapped smugly round myself though my shoulders poke through holes in the fabric and I can't find the needle to sew on the pieces that are missing everywhere. I've tried to bandage my wounds with words from a foreign dictionary I lost before I knew it existed.

Back in my body, I glance at the round No Cameras sign staring at me like a severed eye.

I hear a shout and see the bird man has grabbed Guy's camera with both hands and is pulling, the cord straining around Guy's neck. 'What the hell! Get lost, creep!' He turns, yells, 'Cheryl, help get this freak off me!'

Guy and the eagle are only one metre from me. I could easily take a step and push away the small man, but miraculously my body has turned to stone, is rooted to the earth, unmoving, as if it'd been here for centuries.

The two men locked in a frenzied, jerking tug-of-war when the cord snaps, someone shouts, either Guy or the man, and as if by magic the camera flies up in the air, makes a wide, perfect arc, a form more balanced and symmetrical than anything I've seen in this hurly-burly city, and lands with a splash in the river.

Guy stands slack-jawed. The man has vanished into the chanting crowd, as if he never existed and was something I willed into existence. Guy starts to shout, swear. He turns to me, throws both hands in the air. Indians laugh; then he crouches, his face in his hands. I gaze at the spot where the camera vanished. The water has closed, the wound healed.

Clouds covering the sun part, light flashes down across my body and someone in the sky has taken my picture.

I've never wanted to have children and think now my world will end with me. Have I only been afraid of this? Or do I fear being trapped here on the wrong side of eternity, paradise but a hair's breadth away? Sight not sound imprisons us. It is the eyeball that destroys, sees borders where there are none. About me voices rise and fall, *oma-pada-om.* If I could be reduced to one vast reverberation, the sound of all flesh ringing on forever.

I say, 'Guy, I'll pay for your camera. I'll have to pay Betty for your whole trip and mine. I'm not gonna finish the article.'

In an alleyway, Guy finally speaks. 'Cheryl, I don't understand you at all.'

We stand at an intersection, look at each other. He doesn't touch me.

What remains?

I see Guy's eyes, pale, luminous.

With each step on the grey, cracked concrete, the old thudding song in my heart: I want, I want, I want . . .

Enough

On our first official date you looked deep into my eyes and said, 'You really need to go shopping.'

'Shopping?! What? Is there something wrong with my clothes?' You smirked at my baggy shirt-front. 'Something wrong? When I first met you swimming at the beach, I never dreamt that fully dressed you'd look like a sock puppet,' and you touched my hand.

I wear loose, floppy cotton that doesn't hug my shoulders, clench my pectorals or vise my armpits but allows my muscles to shift and settle. My slim thighs and calves are curtained by tent-trousers that change shape depending on which way the wind's blowing. My sex can hang in this pant leg or in that, and thick, air-bubble-soled shoes safely shield my feet from the hard earth I walk upon. For my muscles are mine. Blood surges through my veins, my heart pounds like a fist in a cage, and saliva fills my mouth and flows swiftly down my throat. The first time we made love back in the bushes by the beach, something in the very centre of me exploded, my lungs fluttered and heaved, my limbs trembled, my groin burned as my lips wandered over the hard surface of your chest, stomach, genitals.

'You're going to have to start dressing better,' you said, 'if you're to be seen with me in the village.'

And so you took me by the hand and led me to Holt Renfrew.

Acres of shirts on racks like a million soldiers standing at attention; mannequins and clerks pointed and preened, while mirrors glimmered everywhere. You dressed me in an olive Versace shirt with seams trimmed with handwoven, herringbone stitching, a puce Armani silk scarf that swirled wave-like up and round my neck, and silver-studded Parasuco jeans that clutched my butt cheeks as if they were two golden apples that could never be let fall. I studied the square, foam-padded shoulders, the shirt stripes you said brought out a hidden, red hue in my face, the French, spiral-embroidered cuffs from which sprouted two pale-skinned hands – yes, I recognized them, they were my own.

Oh how you chattered and laughed in the restaurant afterwards; you broke the biggest pieces of bread and buttered them with the longest knife I'd ever seen. 'You look beautiful in that shirt, just heavenly,' and I began to notice your clothes, the beige, lustrous tie flowing in undulating waves down your smooth, denim shirt that puckered so subtly at the armpit seams whenever you reached for the salt shaker.

Later in your bedroom, things started going wrong. When you removed your clothes, your body suddenly seemed less shapely than the fabric that had covered it. I huddled naked on your cold mattress, equally ashamed of the single-tone colouring of my skin and the pattern-free randomness of the moles and hairs scattered across my torso and legs. We touched each other with vague, hesitant gestures while all around us swelled heaps of multi-coloured clothes throbbing with life.

That night I dreamed mannequins wearing beautiful clothes had taken over the world and were goose-stepping down all the streets of our nation, but, when I tried to speak to them, they'd stop, open their mouths and a faint Styrofoam dust would emerge.

The next morning you and I woke and quickly got dressed.

'Now you've got one good outfit,' you said, 'but a fine, urban gentleman needs several.'

And so you led me further: in and out of designer boutiques specializing in mercerized Ralph Lauren polo shirts; sleek, silhouette Dino Baldini business suits, jacquard boxer shorts and handspun, Ermenegildo Zegna neckties; a tide gathered, rose and I was soon lost in a sea of whirling fabric where sleeveless microcheck Dolce & Gabbana sweaters and knee-zippered Diesel slacks spun in whirlpools, Cerruti satin vests floated in dizzying eddies, white Oscar de la Renta spread wing collars gleamed like coral, and Gucci goat-leather belts thrashed like snakes in fast-moving streams of money.

On the street people stared at us. When I was looking in a shop window, three men approached and discreetly offered telephone numbers, home addresses, invitations to movie-festival cocktail parties – to me, a man barely noticed before. When we entered the village, traffic stopped and men glared from car windows, their smouldering eyes riveted on the small llama ensign just above where my right nipple lay hidden beneath an 80/20 percent blend of cotton and camel hair.

But at night again, our bodies lay lifeless on your bedspread as towering bags overflowed with Dada Damani jeans and Ascot Charez shirts coloured turquoise or champagne; San Rafael blazers bulged through closet doors; print boxers and sheer, fitted T-shirts spilled from dresser drawers that were now too full to close.

That night I dreamed I was trying to undress you but when I removed one layer of clothes, there was another underneath and then another and another. You were a Ukrainian dolls-within-dolls of fabric and I panicked fearing I could never get to the centre of you, until I removed a T-shirt and saw a pinkish swath of skin; I cried out, pressed my lips against it, but then on my tongue, the starch-like taste of Styrofoam.

When I woke in the morning, I wanted to speak with you, but you were already at the mirror, fully dressed.

'Coming?' you said.

'I'm not feeling well. I'd rather stay in today.'

You stared at me for just a moment. You took your credit card from the desk and walked out of the apartment.

I did not put on any clothing. I spent that afternoon on the balcony hammock. I dozed and woke, dozed again. I dreamed of brief flashes in darkness, sludge-filled rivers starting to flow. Then in my ears, a distant thudding.

I did not hear you when you returned.

I only awoke when I heard the gasp of a man about to reach orgasm.

I raced into the bedroom. There you lay naked in a pile of newly-bought clothing, a shirt-tail grazed your nipple, an Armani tie was wrapped round your genitals.

Your eyes met mine and your forehead wrinkled.

'Is it OK?' you said. 'Is this all right?'

'It's perfect.'

I dumped bag after bag of clothes over the now-thrashing body. You licked at labels on shirts, sucked price-tags like lozenges, stuffed a pant sleeve in your mouth while rubbing Banana Republic chinos over your penis. I emptied the dresser drawers, tossed everything from the closet on the bed. Finally the $2,000 Hugo Boss silk suit was left. Only your face was visible at the end of the mound. I let the suit fall on it and immediately heard you exhale wildly.

You'd ejaculated.

I ran naked from your apartment and out onto the street.

Shock waves shot through my torso, as my bare feet slapped on pavement. I raced past fashion boutiques where people pointed and jeered. What in you had reached in me to configure my brain patterns so quickly? You wield an inflatable device that makes my glands empty and fill. I realize the border between us isn't as impermeable as hoped and we march in a vast army without a leader; you blow your whistle signalling 'Charge!' but the sound's an echo of a distant ringing that's hypnotized all of us.

Still, fabric falls like leaves from trees whose roots grasp the ground forever.

I raced into the entrance of Holt Renfrew, leaped up, pulled down a mannequin clad in cargo shorts and smashed its hollow head on the floor.

Shoppers screamed, salesclerks fainted, stacks of boxes collapsed, as security guards rushed towards me, clutched my wrists, pulled me down onto the floor.

I flailed, kicked, bit.

Fluorescent lights shone like searchlights in my eyes.

Do you still want me now, my fierce, glaring lover?

The Whereabouts of Lost Melodies

Hands pass sparkling carafes of *vin rouge*, while words in English, French and German fly through the air like bright-winged insects.

I say to my students, 'I still can't recognize you out of your uniforms.'

'John, the French government sends us to be soldiers eight hours a day only.'

It's the first time they can speak without me correcting grammar and I relish this freedom from duty. I've been teaching them for the past eight months and next week they'll start work as air traffic controllers.

The waiter interrupts, says in French, 'We heard on the radio that the borders are now open and East Germans are entering the city.'

The news descends like a heavy fog. Brows crinkle. Last week Modrow was named the new puppet prime minister of East Germany and the wall encircling West Berlin still seems an eternal European monument, immovable as Stonehenge.

To me all Berlin is frustratingly static, unalterable and, though I've been here a year, impenetrable.

My lone female student mutters, 'I think the waiter can't understand German.' Snickering we plunge into our vanilla mousse, surely more substantial than rumour.

But later when I get on the subway, I see it's packed with people in coal-grey overcoats and boxy, plastic shoes. Women stand pointing at the U-Bahn map, and a bent, elderly man asks me, his German an odd, stop-start dialect, 'Where is downtown?'

'Bahnhof Zoo, sir.'

I eventually get off at Reinickendorf border crossing, race up the stairs and gape at the continuous, oncoming stream of East German Trabant cars flowing through the toothgap opening in the Wall, while above, the iron stop-gate hovers miraculously in mid-air, defying the laws of gravity and politics. On both sidewalks, throngs of

Westerners clap, cheer, some crying, while others dance through the traffic, shaking hands through car windows. Astonished, I see a man jump out of a Trabant and embrace a stranger. The border guards huddle together, smoking, as if to hide their sudden purposelessness.

I run delighted and confused through crowds to Brandenburg Gate, the only place where the Wall has a flat top and see what later becomes the most famous photo of this time: a crowd standing on the Wall. A week before, loudspeakers had blared as police arrested a teenager touching *die Mauer*.

A barrel-shaped man with orange hair helps people up and when I put my foot in his hands, he shouts 'Oi, oi.' I rise, am suddenly on the Wall and feel for the first time that I am not a foreigner, that I have always lived in Berlin, that there's no other place to which I so inextricably belong. People hold each other's shoulders, sing 'Meine Wendy', pass thermoses of *Glühwein* and hot chocolate, a lady embraces a poodle in her lap. In the East, against Brandenburg's pillars, a semicircle of guards; a singing adolescent leaps down, one guard steps forward and politely lifts him back up.

When I get back to my apartment, I phone Tim and say into his answering machine, 'The Wall's fallen, can you believe it? And we're here, actually here!'

A week before, I walked along the border with Tim and Jean-Paul. On the Wall, red-orange paintings of Gumby figures with block feet dissolved into gaudy, chaotic scribblings.

As usual, Jean-Paul spoke non-stop. 'This is why I love Berlin. Everything's ridiculous. This silly park at the centre, those ugly buildings – beside a zoo! I'm so glad I'm out of Paris.'

'I don't really like the city planning,' I said. 'Everything is so … unbalanced. It's depressing.'

Ahead, a decaying, silo-shaped skeleton of a building reminded me of my living situation. If I couldn't find a new apartment by the end of the month, I'd be homeless.

Jean-Paul said exuberantly, 'Ugliness is reality; everything else is kitsch.' He took Tim's hand in his and I was fascinated to see how people ignored them. A woman nonchalantly pushed a stroller past, while three teenagers argued on a bench. Again I told myself moving here was the right decision.

I read: 'Anton Smyth Australia 1985', '*Liebe Jesus*', and in foot-high letters, 'LET ME OUT!'

Over the Wall, faraway apartments of ash-coloured brick stood surrounded by toothpick-shaped cranes. I said, 'They're always building over there.'

'It's an industrial state,' Tim said abruptly, raising his head. 'More corrupt than here but not a hellhole.' I recognized Jean-Paul's words. 'Their vices are obvious; ours, hidden.'

Jean-Paul turned and I saw his hand press Tim's tighter.

When Tim stopped to buy ice cream, Jean-Paul spoke to me quietly. 'Tim is not stupid, you know.'

'I didn't say he was.'

'Though he's American, he's very intelligent. Perhaps other people don't find him attractive; only I can appreciate his qualities.'

On the wall a caricature of Reagan sucking Thatcher's breast.

'It's nice having a day off, eh Tim?' I said.

'For sure. I get sick of that stupid school.'

We turned and headed into the forest.

'Tiergarten!' I said. 'Finally here.' I stopped at the sign. 'Animal Garden, the Animal Garden, that's all you talk about, Jean-Paul. Sometimes I think you *are* the Animal Garden.'

'Am I an animal?' He winked.

'You are a garden.'

We both laughed but Tim kept his head down. Overhead, leaves rustled in the trees. Underfoot, stripes of light across the gravel path. Jean-Paul began humming a tune from *La Traviata*.

Tim said, 'He always sings when he's happy. Mozart releases endorphins in his brain.'

Their banter always fascinated me, as I'd never met such people anywhere else.

'This is the most wonderful place in Berlin,' said Jean-Paul. 'I can't believe John's never been here.' He showed me everything:

THE SOUND OF ALL FLESH

half-concealed trees beside ankle-high piles of condoms, clearings
where people 'do it in fours'. Jean-Paul laughed hysterically, roared
when he saw a soiled handkerchief on a bush. 'When I come here
Saturday nights, there are maybe two hundred men fucking and
nobody cares. The police don't come.' Suddenly he turned to me,
smirked. 'Or maybe you are offended. You are from an Anglo-Saxon
culture. A puritan culture.' His lips were startlingly red and moist,
and his cheeks curved like the sides of two perfectly formed pears.
Why did I keep forgetting he was attractive? 'This is what freedom
is, John.' He smiled wryly. 'Do you not like freedom?'

The day after the Wall falls chaos descends. Line-ups outside banks
merge with supermarket queues, which flow into the sea of people
before the U-Bahn entrance; crowds spill into the roads jammed with
clattering Trabants reeking of singed metal; TV crews from every
country in the world stand on street corners, shoving microphones in
our faces and taking photos of Easterners shopping. About everything there's a hysterical euphoria and I can't help but be infected by
it.

My classes are bedlam. This week I've had a new batch of interested students yet today everybody's late, and no one can concentrate. One man says that last night he actually walked over to East
Berlin and wandered around Alexanderplatz. 'Everything deserted,
like an earthquake had happened.'

A woman says her cousin came over from the East and they pretended it was a birthday, had a party and cake. People heard stories
about sweethearts united, children seeing parents for the first time.

Then Frau Klingner, who three months earlier crossed into West
Berlin illegally, abandoning family, friends and her twenty-year job
as second violinist with the Ost-Berlin Radio-Symphony Orchestra,
cries out, 'None of this will last! It's all a trick by the government.
Everyone will go back and things will be as bad as before!'

By evening the city's transit system is paralyzed, and I have to
walk to my German Improvement class. My teacher runs in, clothes
soaked in sweat, stands at the front of the class and says in her

impeccable *Hochdeutsch*, 'Today German grammar is irrelevant.'
She begins handing out copies of the *Morgenpost*. 'We can only dis-
cuss what has happened. There's no other choice.'

The next morning I gawk despairingly at the empty board in the
apartment-rental agency as the Frau brays, 'Everything was gone by
eight o'clock.'

I can't afford hotels, don't know any people I can comfortably
stay with. There's a campground near the airport and if all else fails
… Still it's zero degrees Celsius at night; I picture myself trembling
on a block of ice as departing planes thunder overhead.

I return to my temporary home, a hospital residence, where I live
with three interns I'm afraid will rat on me. I met the short one, Heinz,
in a bar and when I told him I needed a permanent place, he said, 'You
can come home with me; I won't do anything bad to you.' Non-interns
aren't allowed in the building, and when inspectors visit, Heinz bangs
on my door, 'John, they're here, they're here!' The first time they
came, I locked myself in the bathroom; the next, I ran down the fire
escape in bare feet. Once, in my underwear, I stepped through the
window, onto the adjacent roof and hid behind a chimney. I keep
telling myself: I'm wanted in Berlin, I've got a work visa, they need me
here; but as I lie in bed at night, dread rises, swamps me.

I stand in an endless, zigzagging line at the Central Newsstand; a
truck screeches to a halt, the queue moves forward quickly as people
snatch *Zweite Hands* – the paper with the best flat listings – and run
to the row of telephones opposite, some reserved by waiting friends.
At last I get a phone, receive thirteen busy signals and one 'Flat's
taken, bye.'

That evening I go to a Berlin suburb, Smagendorf, to see my
friend Werner, throw my hands up, cry, 'I'll find nothing! It's impossible now.'

I got to know Werner at the hospital residence, where he'd sometimes visit a friend. As outsiders weren't allowed in, I'd discovered
him politely sitting waiting on the front step.

Today he says, 'You will find an apartment. You must have good
luck.'

For Werner life's a series of simple equations. He and his sister, Doris, live in a dusty flat full of armchairs and stuffed animals, just a block from where they grew up. Werner works in a butcher's at the corner, while Doris is a hairdresser with a white skunk-stripe dyed into her black coif. 'My boss made me do it,' she says in her quaint, measured German. 'He said I looked too boring otherwise.'

We often drink tea and play rummy. Werner will point at a boy on the cookie box, say, 'He looks like you, John!' and we'll giggle. Once we bought an ice-cream cake and ate it in the park, using plastic spoons.

They rarely concern themselves with politics, odd for residents of a city where a wall's in your face. Werner mentions pretty girls he likes but won't approach. 'They'd never go out with me.' Doris has half-hearted affairs she seems to endure out of duty. When I mention my sexual orientation, they just nod silently. Though they're in their twenties, I feel I'm visiting a settled and isolated elderly couple, and amidst the maelstrom of Berlin, their presence is static, stifling and a tremendous relief.

Today Doris speaks breathlessly, 'So many people in the streets and everyone happy.'

Werner went to a border crossing and actually took pictures.

An inspector finally catches me in the kitchen spreading some yogurt on toast. Trembling, I write Heinz a thank-you note, deeply grateful for his uncalled-for kindness to me, a foreigner he barely knew, and drag my luggage to the Seasonal Flat Centre, where people going on holidays rent out vacant rooms in apartments or houses.

As I sit waiting to be called, I think if worst comes to worst, I can always uproot and move home. Something in me violently revolts. Berlin is now the place where the impossible becomes real.

I remember my old apartment in Canada, its shuttered windows and arm-thick radiators. I'd moved to Europe for excitement, a spectacular change. My curiosity still tethers me to the bronze-rimmed café stools of this walled-in city.

The clerk says, 'A man in Wedding is away for a month and his roommate needs someone to pay the missing rent.'

Thus begins my never-ending odyssey from one pretend home to another.

At night I go to bars, amazed I'm still single. I keep thinking a lover will wipe away my frustrations, obliterate my anxieties in the fierce light of desire.

'Berlin is not a city of romance,' says Jean-Paul.

I spend hours at Andreas Kneipe striking up inane conversations with potential suitors. Countless people tell me they're single but have come to Berlin 'for fun. Boring, monogamous types stay in Munich.'

The summer before the Wall opened, I dated an East German. A welder by trade, he'd immigrated here two years ago. I saw him huddled over his beer, taking jerky little gulps, but when I spoke to him, he flung his head back and flashed a huge grin. His hair had rapidly receded though he was only twenty-five.

On our first date he said in his weird, twisting dialect, 'I went home and looked at your country on a map.' He often stared intensely into space, then would suddenly kiss me clumsily and say, 'I like you.'

He insisted we spend our evenings window-shopping. 'Look,' he'd say, 'that gem's worth 8,000 DM!'

At first I found him charmingly ridiculous, but soon he began to wear on me. We couldn't pass a stereo shop, diamond-cutter's or car lot without him stopping to gaze in awe.

'So what if it's a Cadillac!' I said. 'It's only a car.'

'Oh no, in Leipzig you'd never see this.'

I asked him why he came to the West and he was astonished.

'For freedom, of course!'

One day he asked, 'Why do you live in Wedding when there are so many smelly Turks there?' I latched onto this as an excuse to dump him, though everywhere in Berlin, anti-Turk comments fell as continuous as the August drizzle.

'I'm sorry,' I eventually said. 'I think we're too different. But there are other people around who love shopping.'

I think of him when I see a family in plastic shoes tiptoeing down a supermarket aisle, maintaining the respectful silence of visitors to a cathedral. The mother carefully lifts a deodorant stick as if it's a sacred relic, slowly unscrews the top, closes her eyes, sniffs, exhales loudly.

A week after the Wall opens, I sit stiffly on the couch, disturbed by the sudden weight of Jean-Paul's hand on my thigh. It's exciting and I try to ignore it; Tim is shouting angrily at me, 'You're selfish at work! You hog the teachers' books and never share with anyone!'

Lately Jean-Paul has started touching me, patting my butt, making comments about my crotch; he'll blow in my ear and look away. 'Tim and I have an open relationship,' he often says proudly. 'We respect freedom and don't know jealousy. I wouldn't be with someone who was possessive.'

If sex is a plaything for Jean-Paul, he'll be outraged when I reject him. As I'll have to. I know my propensities: after even the briefest sexual encounter, I fall into a pit of longing out of which I can't climb. Besides, Jean-Paul's been such a good friend, why complicate things? I glance down at his smooth hand touched with faint golden hair and feel embarrassed. Is he really after me? It'd be like incest.

'A parasite!' Tim yells. 'Leeching off other peoples' teaching ideas and giving nothing back.'

'That's not true at all,' I protest. I don't understand Tim's new anger.

'Oh c'mon, Tim,' says Jean-Paul. 'You get so mad at John yet if you look, you can see he's very generous.'

Tim says to me sourly, 'Jean-Paul doesn't want to lose the good mood he's had since he fucked some cute guy in East Berlin yesterday.'

West Berliners can now cross to the East without visas or delays, and Jean-Paul and Tim were among the first to go over.

I think back to my only visit. I did everything properly, got a visa, exchanged 25 DM, didn't speak to Russian soldiers or go outside city limits. But in a café a man gave me his address and when I

tried to come back, the border guard said, 'Empty your pockets.'
Right away I was in a 1950s Cold War movie: In a windowless, locked
room the guard grilled me. I didn't know how much to say, not sure if
homosexuality was illegal in East Germany. Finally I said, 'He's just
someone who likes coffee in a coffee shop. I asked him how old he
thought Unter den Linden Street was.'

The guard glared, then let me go. He probably questioned me
because he was bored and had nothing to do, Werner told me later.

Jean-Paul says, 'We took the commuter train past Potsdam
almost to the Polish border. The first time any Westerner could do
this.'

Tim's face softens. 'Yes. It was amazing.'

For a moment our snide, urbane pretensions disappear into the
air. 'It's a wonderful thing that has happened,' Jean-Paul says quietly. 'A wonderful thing.'

Then his hand near my crotch; I shift so his fingers slide down
my thigh, onto my knee. Tim stares into space.

In December the Christmas season is upon us, raucous and colourful
but less glitzy than in North America. I'm living with a divorced
architect. In his fridge, chopped veggies and cheese are exactly
placed pieces of an interlocking puzzle, while glasses stand on
shelves line-perfect as soldiers. When I leave a dishtowel on the
table, he shouts, 'Why have you done this?'

We both start counting off the days to the end of December.

Every month has a repeating, emotional cycle; first, awkward
uncertainty as I get used to new digs and a new housemate, then
mid-month, rising panic as I realize I've got only two weeks left to
find my next place, then the last week blind hysteria as I approach
the black hole that lies after the 31st.

On the 16th I tell the architect I've gotten my *Lichtbescheini-
gung*, a new permit allowing Berlin residents to visit the East without
visas.

He says, 'I will never go there. I don't want them to get my
money.'

The border police are different from before. An anaemic guard jokes about my ID. 'Ah Canadian! You are a lumberjack!'

Yet East Berlin is still East Berlin: the same drab, colourless streets, sooty, egg-carton apartment blocks, rattling trolleys that shake the fillings from your teeth, stark supermarkets stocked with nary an apple but aisles of Bulgarian wine and bottled borscht. East German marks are exchanged three for each Westmark, and I delight in the power conferred on me by the capitalist West.

The Schoppenstube is hilarious. Like a 1950s rec room with bare, plywood walls, ripped vinyl stools, checkerboard floor tiles, and fluorescent lights bright enough for a library. Russian pop tunes crackle from loudspeakers; there's no beer, wine or rum, only vodka flowing clear as water from a curved, copper tap. The people chat, bump shoulders more freely than Westerners, seem friendlier, or maybe the plastic shoes make them less intimidating.

I meet a nurse who says he went to West Berlin on November 9, now a month ago, and was astonished by all the coloured lights; his friend protests, says in a staccato dialect, 'In the West it's all flash with nothing behind.' A university student says most East Germans want material goods rather than the West's true treasures, democracy and freedom from the Stasi. He's afraid that when the proposed reunification happens, the Americans will build a McDonald's in East Berlin's medieval centre.

I encounter a young redhead with terrible dental work. While I talk, he pouts, sighs. When he uses an Eastern idiom I've never heard, he huffs, 'Should we have brought a dictionary?' He grins and I see his crimson gums, blood on the top of his teeth. A vitamin C deficiency?

When I say goodbye, he follows me into the street.

'You can't come home with me; I live in the West.' He trails half a block behind. At the border I say, 'I barely know you. I don't take people home.' He follows me into the booth, shows his ID to the *Zollbeamter*.

He sits silently beside me on the bus in West Berlin and peers into the lit-up street. *Siemens* flashes like a beacon.

We stand by my apartment building. 'I said no to you. Look, I'll give you two marks; the bus stop is over there.'

I approach my doorway, surprised he doesn't follow, turn, watch him slowly walking west, away from the bus stop. He gazes up at the flower-decked buildings on both sides of him, his footsteps echoing down the empty, cobbled street.

Again Tim reminds me he's not really American. 'I left the US eight years ago and have forgotten its lifestyle. Because of Jean-Paul's influence I'm more Parisian now. Jean-Paul says my French is getting great.'

I'm the only friend Tim and Jean-Paul deign to speak English with.

The first time Tim invited me for a drink, he said nonchalantly, 'Yeah, I've got a boyfriend. People find him interesting; he's doing his Ph.D.'

Tim and I had fun together initially, went to several plays, movies and readings before he let me meet Jean-Paul. Shortly after, he said, 'Jean-Paul keeps talking about you; he thinks you're cute and intelligent,' but when Jean-Paul began phoning me, Tim became silent. Jean-Paul still calls me, likes to have long conversations.

Tim would occasionally tell me about Jean-Paul's conquests: 'Three guys in Tiergarten last night. He's savouring the joys of freedom again.' Though Tim was theoretically free to do as he liked, it seemed he was only interested in sleeping with Jean-Paul.

Once Tim asked me, 'If you were seeing someone now, would you be monogamous?'

'I think so. I'm not sure I can fall for more than one person at once. I'd feel pulled apart.'

Surprisingly Tim didn't react like Jean-Paul, who'd snort, call me 'emotionally bourgeois', but said, 'I see.' He began pointing out guys in bars, 'Like him? or him?' and once tried to fix me up with a Cuban guy he'd met in the East but who moved to Hamburg before our first date.

I read the *Morgenpost* daily, even tell my classes, 'I need a permanent place.'

'Who doesn't?' says Frau Klingner.

I discover an ad specifying 'NO FOREIGNERS', and throw the paper to the ground.

But there are times – I'll round a corner in Kreuzberg and surprised, see the Wall, a swinging wrecker's ball, deafening CRASH as the top bricks fall, clouds of dust rise – and the wonder of all that's happening covers everything with a golden light. 'The Wall's fallen, the Wall's fallen!' the words like a kooky nursery rhyme buzz through the air of every kitchen, office and café in cynical, world-weary Berlin.

We've all grasped for reasons – Gorbachev threatened Modrow, or maybe the prime minister became senile – but though there are political causes buried beneath events, it all feels accidental and, I'd be embarrassed to say it, like a miracle. Each Wednesday, wearing a suit, I teach executives at Axel Springer while right outside the window the Wall is gradually transformed from an implacable stone barrier into a row of playfully twisting wires through which tourists wander and children play tag.

'It's a revolution,' the company vice president says to me. At such times I see my own life shrinking to a dot and the external world becoming everything. I joyfully abandon my personal wants and identify solely with History and its unstoppable movement forward.

For the first time in Berlin I see snow. In January, a meagre sprinkling of frail, lost-looking flakes, completely unlike the blinding deluges of my country. Still, I take it as an auspicious sign. Things are about to change for the better.

That evening the Schoppenstube's empty but for one stout, black-haired man who sits examining his vodka-cola.

Sighing at the repetitive monotony of these places, I position myself near the bend of the L-shaped bar. When we make eye contact the third time, he chuckles into a fist.

I say, 'I'm surprised we're the only ones here. Berliners think snowflakes are lightweight bombs falling from the sky.'

'Snow is not dangerous.'

'I'm kidding.' I still can't mimic the sense of humour here.

I move closer and we shake hands. His coarse hair is slicked back and smells pungently of oil. He says his name's Andreas.

I'm surprised and pleased he doesn't ask where I'm from as it's always the first thing.

'Just coming from work, Andreas?' I ask.

'No, I don't work any more.'

I talk lightly. 'Looking for another job?' I wonder how one does that in the East.

He fiddles with a coaster. 'No, I don't think so.' He's squinting, so I change the topic.

He hasn't reacted to my accent. I pause, then test him further. 'In West Berlin a lot of people hate foreigners, Turks, Poles, that's all I hear about. Do you dislike them?'

'Of course not.'

I relax a little. 'So what did you think of the West?'

'I've never been. I don't really want to go actually.'

'Why not?!'

'I'm happy here.' Immediately he becomes interesting to me. Such astonishing complacency and freedom from inquisitiveness! I wonder how he does that, if it's healthy. Perhaps it doesn't stunt but expands him. I have the desire to crack him open like an egg.

As I talk more heatedly, our conversation rises like a wave. When I say, 'You look so German, like a stereotype!' he replies, 'ME?!' and laughs far too loudly, then says, 'If only others thought so too!'

'What do you mean?'

'That's just funny,' he says, wiping his eyes.

At closing time I clutch my drink, finally blurt out, 'Mind if I stay at your place?'

He glares at the label-free coaster. His words come out slowly. 'I would like that. But you must sleep on the couch. Is that OK?'

Anything is OK. My heart pounds double for each step we take on the crumbling sidewalks.

Furniture's easily available in East Berlin, and I don't know why his apartment's so spartan, only a mattress and several large cardboard boxes filled with books, paper, clothes.

Contrary to what we'd agreed, Andreas jumps me. But when my fingers slide beneath his underwear elastic, he snatches my hand, stands up, 'No,' he nervously reaches for his pants.

'What?! Are you ...' I hesitate, 'not healthy?'

'I'm fine.'

'Maybe you've got no genitals like Barbie or Ken?' I realize he doesn't get the reference. 'It's OK. Maybe next time.'

He looks away, says, 'All right.'

In the morning he gives me his phone number, which is useless as there are few lines between East and West Berlin. We agree to meet on Saturday.

At the door, suddenly – and it's completely unnecessary – he embraces me, says, 'I'm sure you are a good person.'

Walking down the street, I think this is the arrival of freedom, the unheralded miracle bursting forth in my own life. I tell myself not to get overexcited but on the U-Bahn going home, I see Easterners toasting each other with Western *Glühwein* and can't help feeling one with them.

'YOU CAN'T FREE THE GOOD WITHOUT RELEASING THE BAD.' The *Morgenpost* had predicted the reappearance of right-wing extremists.

I'm eating a ketwurst in Lenin Square when ten men with shaved heads and swastika armbands march past shouting, 'Foreigners! Leave Germany!' My body stiffens with outrage though I know their hatred isn't really directed at me for my skin is too white.

The next week the right-wing Republikaner set up a stage opposite my workplace and as a man in lederhosen bellows through a bullhorn, protesters half drown him out by blowing scream-like whistles.

THE WHEREABOUTS OF LOST MELODIES

I'm teaching the future tense and hear isolated phrases 'Africans taking jobs … Germany soon one true nation … the foreigners go! …'

February. My next roommate, Hanjo, trembles when he speaks, can't look me in the eye, only leaves his room to use the toilet, and at first I assume he's a pushover. Yet one day he screams, 'You are like panther prowling in my apartment.' That afternoon a note on my door: 'Get out by 5:00. Hurry.'

Horrified I bang on his door. 'Hanjo? I must leave here? Is this serious?'

His small voice, 'I'm a nervous wreck with another person around.'

The words tear from the back of my throat, 'But what about me?! I've got nowhere to go!' Then intelligently, 'And how can you afford the rent alone?'

A long silence as I wait on his threadbare rug. The door opens a crack; his one visible pupil dilates, and he shouts. 'You must pay 100 DM more! Or you leave now!'

Thus begins the cycle of fights-threats-payment. Each round of his hysteria costs me 50 DM; I'm being duped but feel powerless.

My room has no lock and I soon discover money missing from my backpack. I continue searching for another apartment and once during a screaming match burst into tears.

Hanjo's impressed, says, 'Next time you must get a written contract before moving in with someone.'

Finally one morning I refuse. 'I've got two more weeks here and I'm paying nothing more.'

That evening I arrive to see my few belongings in garbage bags on the sidewalk. The lock on the door's been changed. Hanjo is nowhere.

I sleep in Werner's kitchen, then on Tim's sofa. I fantasize: Hanjo is walking by the Wall, a chunk falls and crushes him; or he's at Brandenburg Gate, jumps into the semicircle of soldiers who get confused and shoot him.

Jean-Paul has stopped touching me but now always hovers right beside me. I turn and he is trying to blow in my ear. 'You are so sensitive to other people's behaviour,' he says seriously, 'fragile like a flower, charmingly hesitant and afraid of contact. That's why you're single; your vulnerability challenges people.'

I swing round to see Tim shuffling behind, head down, dog-like. He looks up and I notice his gnawed lips. I realize that Jean-Paul knows many people (a new guy every night) but I'm the only person he sees almost as frequently as Tim.

We stand studying the photos in the Checkpoint Charlie Museum.

'Berlin is now the centre of the world,' Jean-Paul says. 'Elsewhere people feel the repercussions of what's happening here. Tim and I wanted to move to Spain next year, but not now.'

We look at the famous photo of the East German border guard who defected to the West when the Wall was being built. His arms are wide open, a rifle falling from one hand as his body hovers in mid-air above the whirling loops of barbed wire.

'Tim and I heard a woman from your country on the radio today, John. It was hilarious. Some French writer has written a book about an old man having sex with a very young girl and this Canadian woman was screaming, "Oh, it's so terrible, only in Paris would they publish such a book." I think she's part of this new movement from America. You just glance at someone's ass without written permission and deserve to get your penis chopped off. Ridiculous!' A woman at the Wall holds a baby above her head so his father on the other side can see. 'Free your mind and take delight in a good fuck; that's the best philosophy.'

As we leave the museum, Jean-Paul takes both our hands and we walk as a threesome, past the ruins of the Gestapo headquarters, the small hillock where Hitler's bones are buried. When we see the Tiergarten, Jean-Paul flinches and we turn back. Last Saturday skinheads converged on the park's gay section and beat in one guy's head with a car jack.

At eleven-thirty in Pool Disco, a dark, swelling sea of shirtless, tattooed dancers, non-stop strobe lights slice their movements into disconnected fragments; Jean-Paul vanishes into a haze of cigarette smoke and dry ice. A bar stool vibrates rhythmically against my leg as Tim watches, biting his lip.

Unexpectedly he says, 'OK, John, you can do what you want now.'

'What?'

'Touch me, whatever. I know what you want.'

My mind does a complete three-sixty. Is the music too loud? When he winces, I see he's serious. Silver light flashes across his lips, his large oval eyes pleading, I'm lost, take me home. 'John, I know how you watch me at work.'

I can't speak for a whole minute. 'Look, Tim, you're a nice person but I've never watched ... You are handsome, I find a lot of people attractive and ... I enjoy being friends with you and Jean-Paul but I've never been interested ... in you ... like this.'

He looks down and I feel I've slashed his face with a switchblade. 'If you would do something nice for me,' he says. I'm incapacitated with embarrassment. 'I'd ... just like you ... to let me ... kiss you.'

We are free from jealousy. Jean-Paul and Tim's motto. Yet still ... is Tim completely my friend? ... I choose to believe, yes. But ...

Yellow light on his cheeks, his eyes are craters. I know he's often lonely. As I am. Tim and I are more similar than I've admitted.

'All right,' I sigh. 'Do it then. If it'll make you feel better.'

My eyes shut and immediately his tongue's in my mouth. I realize this is the only time anyone has really kissed me like this in Berlin, and when our mouths separate, I impulsively embrace, hold him for a minute. I feel I might start crying.

We stand apart and he darts into the crowd.

Later when I meet Jean-Paul at the coat check, his cheeks are flushed. On the street he says abruptly, 'Did you have an enjoyable evening? What in particular did you enjoy?' then hisses in my ear, 'What do you think of Tim?'

'Well ... I like him, he's my friend.'

In Hugos Ufer, Tim talks animatedly about the Polish market. 'Now each morning hundred of Poles cross the border and stand in the muddy field at Potsdamer where they sell shit from home, broken alarm clocks, ripped bedsheets. I saw one guy holding a spoon and shouting, 'One mark' over and over.'

Suddenly Jean-Paul grabs and holds my arms so my face is right before his. 'Tim said you two were French-kissing and then you started hugging him!'

I pull myself loose, say, 'Well, kind of,' then 'Jesus Christ, what's with you two?'

Jean-Paul is silent for a good while. Then for the first time in months he speaks German. 'I'm reminded of that time we talked about English and you got so angry. Remember? How I said English has simplistic conjugations, chaotic preposition use, and nothing self-reflecting in the language. When someone with a natural intelligence is born into this tongue and has every thought based in it,' he looks straight into my eyes, 'it is tragic.'

Jean-Paul and Tim observe me across a great distance. For a moment I realize how foreign they are to me. How did I ever think I knew them? I speak sadly in my own language. 'I don't accept what you've said.'

On Saturday I wait outside Andreas's flat. Every five minutes I pound on his door though I know he's not in. I give up pressing the timed-light button and sit on a stair in the dark. Eventually I scribble a note, 'If you don't want to see me, just say so,' and stuff it under his door. I kick the wall once.

Another hall door opens and a woman sticks her head out. She says, 'He's left. He and his parents moved to Israel. They think Berlin's too frightening now.'

I share an apartment in the industrial section of Kreuzberg, the closest I've ever lived to the Wall. My roommates, a young woman and her teenaged boyfriend, are both deaf, so we communicate by writing. I like the way this slows life down. By the end of each evening the kitchen's littered with torn sheets of paper. At night they make love in the next room and have no idea how noisy they are. The sound blends with the roar from the trains shunting along the new line to the East. I press the pillow over my head, muttering trains-sex, trains-sex, and fall asleep.

In my German Improvement class everyone is arguing about the new laws for foreigners. A Latvian man yells, 'It'll be worse; everyone knows. Even Cuban immigration to East Germany is down.'

On our break a Kurdish woman asks me, 'And John, why are you in Berlin?'

'Berlin has long been surrounded by a wall,' I say. 'I'm fascinated by borders, the line where one thing becomes another. Besides, I studied German in university.'

She stares blankly. Both her brothers were killed in rebellions in Turkey. 'So, you're a ... tourist?'

'OK. I'm a tourist.'

That afternoon, strolling through Tiergarten, Werner, Doris and I discover three floppy sunhats perched on an overfull trash can; we each put one on and dance about, mugging like snot-nosed aristocracy, then fling them away like Frisbees when Werner finds a worm in his. We collapse onto a bench laughing. I realize my happiest moments in Berlin have been with Werner and Doris and wonder why I don't spend more time with them.

I watch my friends pulling fruit from their rucksacks, and recognize that it will be hard to leave.

Werner announces he might go to a college in Munich soon, and I am floored. 'Everything is changing,' he says. 'Maybe I must change.'

'I don't think he should go,' says Doris.

'Would you like it, Werner? You know nobody there.'

'John, you came here alone. Maybe I have to leave and see something new.'

I don't say this but I'm learning that the line between neurosis and desire for change is very thin.

In July the two currencies are united.

Change continues at a breakneck pace. Bus lines now run across the border, all the East's subway stations are opened, the French, British, American and Russian armies have been asked to leave, and the streets are packed with refugees flooding in from former Eastern Bloc countries.

Romanian gypsies, heads swathed in dirty, striped handker-chiefs, dance for money in Breitscheidplatz as their children forage in trash cans; young Poles on street corners sell contraband Hungarian cigarettes, and busloads of American and Japanese tourists have descended like locusts to pick clean the remaining crumbs of the Wall and buy up now-obsolete Russian army uniforms, plaster Lenin busts and other Communist kitsch.

Hatred for the old prime minister has become endemic. My East German students say that Honecker, though ailing in some decaying Leipzig hospital, and his wife, Margot, the Marie Antoinette of the East, must be visibly made to suffer.

Frau Klingner no longer talks of the concerts she gave with her Ost-Berlin Orchestra before illegally emigrating here. 'I finally walked over to East Berlin yesterday,' she says, 'I saw the lights on in my old house. Someone was living in my house!'

Bicycle Dreams

I wear a muzzle I can't remove.

Zachary's talking merrily, his mouth opens and closes; his unhooked tie hangs like a viper from the chair back.

He smiles at my tofu, this piece of moon on his fork. 'So I said, "I'm seeing a guy already," and he looks at me ...'

He likes the new arrangement, my lips clamped shut, his own words, censored. It's to end the old fights. He got tired of me yelling at him, and now it's all off limits: my articles, discussions with friends. 'We get arguing about these abstract things,' he'd said, 'that have nothing to do with us.'

I do believe him.

However. Inside me, words, sentences, whole paragraphs are pressed against a chink in the wall.

I dare to say, sounding casual, 'Do you like my place?'

'Sure. It's cool, Redge. Small but neat. It reminds me of a university residence. And that,' he points to the multi-coloured boxes, 'is amazing. Is this part of some government study?'

I clench my jaw. 'No. I'm doing it because I want to. The green is for plastics, the red, glass, the white's for paper.' I watch his face. Does he want to do likewise? Light dances in his eyes, his eyes, his beautiful grey eyes. At times he'll touch me so gently and when he'll turn and say my name, something bursts inside me. But still ...

'What're those worms in the glass box?' he asks.

'They eat the biodegradable waste.' I must look away from him. 'They're very easy to use. Everyone could use them, but of course people are lazy. You know, the hole in the ozone would –' I stop, feel the ropes wrapped round me. Shit! I say quickly, 'Could you live like this?'

He chuckles, 'No,' my hand clenches the fork. 'I'd feel embarrassed 'cause it's so small. What if I had my boss over?' I see his round, beaming face, sharp, bookend sideburns, fascinating cleft chin, his delicate ears that (it always astonishes me) so eagerly take in my diatribes. 'I mean, no offence, Redge. Of course I like it 'cause it's yours, your life is so wild, it flips me out. Just like I always say, I find you very unique.'

I stare at this intruder in my apartment. Zachary is a rock that can be sculpted into nothing but himself; he can't even feel threatened here. He'd said he used to be like me. Am I a piece of melting wax, softening and being lost forever? The fear of metamorphosing into my enemies has been a bass note droning all my life.

'You know, me and my ex-wife used to go to amusement parks for thrills,' he says. 'Like Canada's Wonderland. The rides were really fun for us, especially the log flume! You feel like you're travelling in a log in an African river when really it's a cylinder in a metal trough with fake palm trees everywhere. Ha! We used to like the ice cream there too, homemade and in all these different flavours. I'd eat three or four at once, but I had such high-stress days, I could burn it off – or so I liked to think.' He shrugs and pats his belly. 'It's funny now when I think I believed those little trips were special. "Working outside the box" as guys at the office repeat *ad nauseum*. Maybe I was denying what I really wanted in life 'cause for originality, compared to you, Redge, all that's nothing.'

I am smiling, though I wish I weren't.

He stands and comes behind me. 'Thanks for the grub, dude.' A warm hand presses my shoulder, lips touch the side of my neck, stubble grazes my skin, hot breath in my ear, with a will of its own my neck arches back, one hand presses his face against me and I slip and slide down a dark tunnel, am lost, my words flung like confetti to the wind.

At night I dream I'm kissing Zachary while sun rays slice the ground; ochre-tipped boils erupt from every pore on my body; the Earth whirls in space, a shrivelling peach pit, and from my very centre, panic screams like a siren.

The next day in my mail slot, *Natural Life*, the headline: 'Hole Over Antarctica Now the Size of the US'. I see a similar article in the *Toronto Star*, a small box on the back page.

I carry my month's garbage (it all fits in a pocket-small packet) and place it beside the mountain of plastic containers discarded by the office building next door.

Zachary's car is a monster that's swallowed us. We sit in its belly and watch the dying world through the front windshield. Rain splatters and wipers squeak. One day: car, the next: public transit. This was our agreement, my compromise. When we pass a cyclist, my hand grips the armrest. Don't hit that angel-on-wheels! I lower my eyes, wonder if I'm absurd. I turn and see my reflection in the glass, translucent, my face blurred.

Have I annoyed everyone yet? Have my self-righteous fantasies, as integral to me as the sludge in my bones, caused all to turn away in horror?

Zachary nervously drums the steering wheel.

'What's wrong?' I say.

'I hope it works out today.'

'Just because I live in a basement doesn't mean I'm socially inept. I thought you said this girl was an artist.'

She has a jewel in her nose and talks about kabuki theatre. I saw a performance once and give her my opinion. Zachary watches me, his face lit; the sun glows in his skull. The sides of my lips start to curl to a smile, my heart pounding – imbecile! His approval shouldn't matter.

Still, when the artist says, 'Artaud was a mastermind of deception …'. Zachary squints, lost, and I reach under the table and touch his knee reassuringly.

Going home he says, 'When you went to the restroom, she said all the things I love about you. You're serious, so well-informed, you have intense eyes. I should introduce you to my colleagues. Our workplace is gay-positive, do you have a suit?'

Wearing the Devil's uniform, I descend to Hell and shake hands with Lucifer's apostle, Zachary's boss, Mr Fent, president of Reed Advertising, purveyor of lies, treachery and brainwash. My tongue is nailed down with ten-ton bolts. Cardboard words fall from my mouth and everyone laps them up. I know I'm half-ridiculous, insane: if I think these people are cardboard cut-outs, then I am too. Still I feel resentment like a hard stone in my chest.

Zachary says, 'I felt so proud of you. How'd you know about country clubs? Is that from your parents? One of the secretaries called you a dreamboat. "So hunky," she said.'

The car hood's down and the wind wildly whips Zachary's hair, as multicoloured neon streams over him. He eyes the screeching fleet of passing motorcycles, the electrified skyscrapers, distant smoke stacks half-lit below the moon.

I wonder how it feels when you think the world's not against you, when life flows through you and you don't judge it.

I feel I'm stepping to a cliff-edge.

I can take no more and must act. I've put a bomb in his birthday card that could explode in our faces.

'Here you go.' I kiss his cheek. 'Happy birthday!'

He opens and reads. '"Special present for you outside." Oh!' He's giddy as a child on Christmas. 'What is it?'

I summon strength, and think, 'Be innocent.' My eyes become bright. 'Remember last week.' I'm smiling. 'You said to Margot that you're out of shape, you wanted to start ... but you didn't have ... well, so you see, I bought you,' I sing merrily, 'a bike!' His smile slowly collapses, and his eyes darken. He stares at me, searching but my mask doesn't crack. 'We can go cycling on the boardwalk together. You always hated how I'd go off on my own.'

He watches, then his cheek muscles relax. 'You're right. It's an awesome gift!'

Heading outside he says, 'You didn't spend too much on this, did you, Redge?'

I keep my head down, too ashamed to look at him.

'No, it's just a cheap, second-hand thing,' which is true. When I see Zachary tentatively touch the handlebars and press the tires, I want to weep with joy. 'Cyclists are road vermin,' he'd said. 'Oh, they say, "We're great, we're the ones who help the environment," but their brains are stuffed with trail mix. They're always at fault in accidents.' I'd complained and he apologized; still he wouldn't believe cyclists were the most concerned and responsible, 'the most moral', I almost said. Zachary said, 'We car drivers put up with cyclists' shenanigans,' and now here he was, ready to ride with me.

'Let's go cycling on Saturday,' I say.

'OK,' and he smiles at me so trustingly, I feel a stab of guilt – he can't see how I manipulate him. I brush aside the feeling.

At night his smooth chest presses mine, my tongue probes his mouth, and I realize: I'm thinking only of him right now. Not necessarily a good thing.

Later we lie silent, as stripes of sunlight lengthen along the bedspread; the rising roar of traffic builds to a peak as the old sentences whiz through my head:

My emotions (love, lust …) are ephemeral, clouds crossing the sun, but garbage is concrete, piling up along curbs daily.

From Zachary's car pollutants ascend and gobble at the sky, yet he thinks I'm crazy, and maybe I am.

Still, he can't help the way his mind's made, his upbringing made him Zachary, as mine made me Redge. And certainly he'd never change me, has never wanted to, so why not enjoy him?

And if I dumped him and he were seeing someone else, he wouldn't change for the better.

I rarely meet people who share my opinions, have never met such a gay person – homos are hopelessly bourgeois – Zachary's so fine otherwise, perhaps he's the best life offers.

How much effect can he – or I – have on the world anyway?

Why do I fear him?

Zachary stretches and cries out groggily, 'Cubicles, cubicles, cubicles! I live in an office cubicle.' He gets up, showers, returns, a bit of toothpaste foam in the corner of his mouth. 'I can't wait till I have my own office next month, Redge. Yesterday my sister dropped by and said me and my colleagues looked like we were lined up like pigs at a trough. I was so bored I started hanging bright red ribbons on my computer to keep me awake. I should wrap one round the new boss's mouth.' Chuckling, he takes a white shirt from his wardrobe. 'Last week she came in when we were all doing synchronized dusting and told us to knock it off.' He picks up a striped tie. 'Luckily I got some clients today and get to be out of the office – I know, I'm on a treadmill, but I'm there of my own free will and so can't complain if I fall off.' He does a slow-motion pantomime of a man whirling his arms as he falls to the ground. He snatches up his tie, snaps it in the air.

On the radio another pollution-warning: '... the elderly and asthmatic should stay inside ... please only use cars or lawnmowers if absolutely necessary.'

Outside a bumper-to-bumper gridlock. Just another day.

We stand by the glimmering lake. My bike seat presses snugly into my butt, the stiff crossbar touches my knee.

I say, 'I'll ride to that post and wait for you. I know you haven't done this in years.'

I press the pedals and glide beneath trees, my wheels whirr quietly. When I stop and turn, I see Zachary jerking the handlebars, the bike wobbling like a huge egg on a spoon, his brow's knit, his mouth twisted.

Never had I loved him as much as then.

He reaches me and I want to grab, kiss him, but there are families nearby, and he'd be horrified.

He says, 'Well, this'll be good exercise for me.'

We ride together all afternoon, down trails that twist and turn like a huge child's doodle. Seagulls call back and forth. We laugh going over streams, through the hair of lakeside willows. Ontario Place, its gleaming ball and labyrinthine towers, rises miraculously from the water. Distantly, on the highway loop, cars move in silence as if behind glass: a bad dream we've woken from. The warehouse district is abandoned; our shouts echo down the ghost-town streets. We hurtle down Lakeshore hill like runaway horses and collapse laughing beneath an oak tree.

The sun drops from its zenith; the car ride home is imminent, then – I can't stop myself. I turn to Zachary, who's pointing at a distant beach, talking, his face and shirt drenched. '… at the top of that cliff there's a pipe spitting sewage into the lake, and when I was a kid, my friends and me would come down and dare each other to stand on it. I did that a million times. It's funny, Redge, but we only thought of how bad your foot would smell if it touched the discharge but didn't ever think of how dangerous it was to stand on a pipe thirty feet above the ground. The weirdest thing was last summer my company had their picnic at that other beach there and while I was schmoozing with the vice prez, I turned and saw that childhood pipe in the distance. You wouldn't believe how freaky that was, Redge. Like seeing my childhood and adulthood smushed together, the past and present, or like the twilight zone, with two worlds colliding.'

'Zachary,' I say. 'Why don't we ride up University. There's a neat park I can show you.'

'University?!' He looks at his bike, then over at me. 'I think that's too difficult. These bike paths are a challenge for me. I mean, that's a real road!'

'Oh, I'm confident you can do anything.' I laugh and then smile with real warmth.

His mouth is a diagonal line. 'Well … I guess if you think I can.'

It's OK. It'll be good for him.

'Let's go then. And take care.'

As I cruise along the street, my pedals make beetle-like clicks. I hear the creaking of Zachary's bike a distance behind.

Now he'll understand. He'll see the way things are.

Skyscrapers loom like canyon walls around the turbulent river of traffic. Horns blare; exhaust fumes reek. As I pedal, cars fly by like hurled boulders; taxis shoot past like sharks. Nothing will hit me. I feel bold and defiant, a bullet aimed at our civilization's heart.

At a stop light I turn back to see Zachary slowly pedalling, his forehead's ridged, his dark eyes bulge.

I wonder if I should stop, check to see if he can manage. But no, the light turns green, and I speed on. We cross King, Queen, Dundas;

I wait for him at each intersection. I start to relax – it all becomes so fun. Then as I leave Chinatown and am approaching College – without warning – far behind, tires shriek, a horn, a woman screams. I look back: a car stopped in the intersection; beneath a front wheel, a bike; on the pavement, a body – Zachary.

I cry out and ride back.

Zachary lies shaking, blood on his cheek.

In the ambulance I hold his hand. I try to be strong but, 'Oh Zachary, I'm so sorry. I knew that trip would be dangerous but ...'

His eyes turn in their sockets, glare at me.

I sit in the waiting room and watch the line of doctors getting coffee in disposable, Styrofoam cups. Suddenly I'm incensed, I stand, scream, 'Look at you all! Those cups have CFCs in them and'll destroy the ozone layer! You know it, you're educated people, you have no excuse, and you're all sending the world to hell!' Silence. People stand stiffly and don't move. Shaking, I collapse on my chair, put my face in my hands. For a second I wish I were a simpler person who didn't care about things. Yet I remember my articles, all the doors I've knocked on, the people I've fought, and I tell myself: If I lapse, no one else will do the work.

The doctor says, 'He's fine. But he's lost a lot of blood, and his arm is broken in three places.'

I make myself smile when I enter the room.

'Well, how do you feel?'

Zachary is silent. When he stares at me, I look down.

He says, 'I'm OK.'

'Your bicycle ... it's a pretzel.'

'Yeah,' he says. 'I'm not gonna get a new one.'

I sit beside him and put my head on his pillow. Then I begin sobbing. He puts his free arm on my shoulder and I listen, wish he'd speak. I realize, almost not believing myself, what it is that I'd really like him to say:

Honey, I'm obsessed with biodegradable products.

I can't sleep thinking of ozone depletion.

Together we'll reverse the greenhouse effect.

If Zachary can't commit himself to the Earth, how could I believe he'd commit himself to me?

'There, there,' he says coldly. 'There, there.'

I don't know if I can bear the look in his eyes when I tell him I'm leaving.

We're in a car heading north, my bike on the roof. We'd seen each other so little since the accident; we both claimed to be busy. And now Zachary phones me, wants to spend the day by a lake up north swimming or rather, wading. His cast is still on.

The drive is long, but our words are few. When I speak, I'm reaching into dark water, trying to find warm spots. Zachary's words are gentle; there are open spaces between sentences. Zachary loves starting over. For him life is a series of beginnings with no ends. But I have a hatchet raised that I should let drop. Sunlight through the pines flickers in my eyes; light flecks flash across my body.

'See,' says Zachary, 'there's lots of beaches along these lakes. When you see one you like, just tell me.'

White sand and parked cars, children playing with buckets. Soon the trees become thin, branchless. Forests of toothpicks pointing at the sky and there, a lake the colour of shaving cream.

'Stop!' I say. 'I want off here.'

'Here?'

'Yes.'

'But it's –'

'There's the parking lot.'

He brings the car to a reluctant stop.

'Let's go,' I say, leaving the car. The beach is studded with tar-paddies.

'Wait a minute. I don't want to spend the afternoon here!'

I remove my clothes, pull on my bathing suit, put one foot in the water.

'You're not going swimming in that!'

I turn to him and say, 'Yes, I am.' I take a deep breath. As I speak, my self-image reassembles itself, a Polaroid figure slowly takes shape and becomes fully formed. I gesture towards the water. 'This is real life. Those other beaches are lies, exceptions.' The locked-up words burst from me. 'This is what we're doing, especially you with your advertising job, brainwashing people into buying junk that'll fill up landfill sites and choke the earth,' I love the sound of my old words '– and buying cars, the destroyers of the planet.'

'Oh man!' He turns away and sighs loudly. 'Are you back on that again?' When he moves his arm, his cast swings like a club. It hurts my eyes so I look down. 'Can't you ever forget all that? Has it ever occurred to you for once to have fun in life?'

I wade into the lake. 'These things are important, not ...' I want to say 'not us' but can't.

'C'mon, Redge, don't be like this. I was hoping this could be a ... we can get to know each other again.' Then he says, 'I missed you these past few weeks.'

I swish the water with my hand. 'I'm just a walk on the wild side for you.' Do I believe this? I force out the words, 'And you're lazy. All car drivers are, especially those like you who've heard the truth and refuse to accept it ... Once I took up an environmentalist lifestyle, I realized I could do anything.' Yes, I want clarity, no more push-pull feelings inside me. 'Unlike brainwashed assholes like you, I go places on my own steam, not by shitting gas fumes into the atmosphere. You stay the car pig you are. I'm not hiding from reality.'

I dive into the lake. The warm, oily water rushes across my face, arms, legs. For a moment I'm suspended touching nothing, no fish, plants, or even algae. I come up, press my feet into the soft bottom and look back.

Zachary has placed my bike on the beach. He drops my backpack beside it. He shouts, 'OK, Mr Know-it-all Bike Man, if you can do anything, get home without me!'

He enters his car. The engine roars. From the window he takes one fleeting look at me. Then he's gone.

I stand completely still. The water feels cold. I slowly wade to the shore.

* * *

I'm sitting on the beach wrapped in a towel. I've eaten my last granola bar. The sun is setting. I'll sleep here tonight.

A quick inhale, and I put my face in the crook of my arm. Zachary and I had met in an intersection. He cut me off, and I screamed in his window, 'Do you want a fucking bike lock in the head?' My wheel had gotten bent, and I made him take me to a repair shop. 'You shouldn't be driving a car.' I lectured him all the way. 'And I'm a homosexual,' I yelled. 'I guess you don't like that either!' After he paid, he looked me in the eyes and said, 'Are you free Saturday night?' I was confused. For once my words had no power. They did not repel him and – I couldn't forget this – they weren't what attracted him.

I looked at him. His eyes were on me. I said yes.

I fall back on the sand. The last sun rays touch my face. 'But it all was –' I cry, 'a bicycle dream!'

The world is a head with a hole kicked in it; brains leak into the atmosphere.

If there were some part of me, an unused kidney or stray bone unlinked to everything and inextricably pure.

I'm not Jesus Christ, don't have the hormones to grow a decent beard and am exhausted by self-sacrifice. Do my desires count for anything? If I'm driven to save the Earth, there must be something on it worth saving. These cascading images must add up to something.

Around me, trees point like fingers towards the sky. A torrid energy has always burned at the centre of me and I've frenziedly clutched at the world so it won't slip away forever. But what's my place in everything? Every day the sun rises in the east but there's nothing to tell you it'll eventually set in the west and it could just stop of its own free will, directly overhead, at the twelve o'clock position, and stand blazing down on you forever.

The sand grows colder. Wind whistles through dead branches. The lake smells like sulphur.

I hear a car, the crackle of wheels on gravel. The engine moan dies.

The door clicks open, shuts. He stands, shadowed beneath trees.
I run towards him, we embrace and collapse into the earth, my face on his stomach.

The next day we head home.

Zachary does not put his hand on my knee. I gaze at his profile etched sharply in the window's pale light. Then we both look straight ahead.

Rows of factories announce the city limits. Cars roar round us like bees lost in a huge hive. Smog forms a canopy above.

The Modesty Wrap

Mt Ararat was only sixty miles away, but I was not well enough to go. My skin felt oversensitive, as if it'd bruise when touched. An hour after eating, in my stomach, I could feel a fist opening and closing. I stood on the edge of Lake Van. Sharp-toothed gravel dug into the soles of my feet, as, before me, boys and men bounded through water. Beaches were the only places in Eastern Turkey where one could be semi-undressed in public. A wave crashed and the men's white ribbed briefs and T-shirts glowed translucent in the water.

In ten minutes it'd be 5 p.m. and the swimmers would be spirited away, vanishing like mist. Soon after, the village would let mango rinds, overripe olives, the day's excrement flow down Pidin stream into this lake where, my guidebook assures me, 'the alkaline content is the highest in the world. Lake Van is self-cleaning and harmful bacteria disappear instantly. Delighted tourists can create suds in the water without any soap.' The men's movements accelerated, urgently outpacing the normal rhythm of my life. I took one step forward and a wave smelling of dew-flower petals washed up and around my foot.

Then on the breeze a voice calling. I turned and viewed the plain littered with bulbous rocks lying like pulled teeth. On a hill stood two figures waving; their hair billowed in the wind. Women? No woman had spoken to me in three months as though they'd disappeared into an unseen netherworld where they polished tessera-tile or embroidered kilims. My body suddenly felt strangely alert. I began moving towards them. As I neared, I thought the women were Germans who'd failed to cross the rifled border into Iran, and were left to linger and perish here in the uncharted backwaters of Eastern Turkey.

Oddly, the woman were wearing trousers and cotton shirts. They were young – my age – and had silver belts round their thin waists. Their pants looked slightly stained, but were snug and seemed ironed. One woman opened her mouth but said nothing. A horizontal crease ran across the middle of her nose – she reminded me of a girlfriend I'd had in high school. I noticed the bump of a brassiere-strap pressing into the fabric of her shirt. I swept one hand through my hair and cleared my throat. Unconsciously I brought my hand to my neck as if checking the knot of one of the executive ties my father makes me wear.

The woman said in English, 'Nice to meet you,' stuttering the t's, definitely Turkish.

The other said, 'Come.'

I followed them past collapsing wood shacks and gleaming orange stucco buildings covered with interlocking geometric designs. Chickens scattered, dust rose as our feet pounded against parched earth. We passed a man crouched praying on a chequered mat, bare-foot children in gutters shouting 'Where you from?', an ebony-shawled old woman on a donkey, a man balancing a huge platter of stacked bread-rings on his head.

Both women had dark, sun-streaked hair, round shoulders, breasts petite, the way I like them. We reached the top of a cliff and sat looking over the water. Though small, from here the lake looked as if it stretched from one side of the world to the other.

The women were surprised when I said I came from New York City.

They asked why I was in Turkey, and I answered, 'I'm going to Mt Ararat.' A song in my head:

> I'm going to Mt Ararat
> Mt Ararat, Mt Ararat
> I'm going to Mt Ararat
> Where the Earth will touch the moon.

'I've been travelling in Turkey a long time. Two months, but it seems longer.'

I asked them where they were from, and one said, 'Izmir.'

'That's far from here. Why have you come to Van?'

'Our father has died,' said the woman. 'We have come to pay our respects.' And with that they turned and looked out over the water once again.

My body had taken on a life of its own and refused to listen to me. For weeks I'd wandered smugly through throngs of Westerners who vomited into open-pit toilets or moaned in hostel beds as they waved bottles of Pepto Bismal or Pexdryal like magic amulets that refused to work. Restaurants were battlefields where only I survived. My body was an invincible iron tank firing on armies of toxins seen approaching on distant plains. But somewhere on the imaginary line separating modern Western Turkey from the wild East, there had been a salad of unwashed vegetables or perhaps an uncooked shish kebab from a sidewalk vendor. In Van I awoke vomiting. Now I subsisted on a monk's diet of yogurt, bread crumbs and tea. At times there was a pressure in my bowels, and as I crouched balancing on the raised, metal footholds of pit toilets, I imagined an evil force rushing from my body.

Nearby, Mt Ararat towered above the arid plain like a hallucination. There, five worlds collide: Turkey, Iran, the USSR, the sky and the cosmos. Mt Ararat has the highest ground-to-summit distance of any place on earth. Its slope is like a bridge to the sky, and you feel you can walk up and off the Earth. In its brooding forests are shrouded caves of rifle-toting terrorists; escaping Soviet refugees forever run through its woods but never escape; above, blinding-white glaciers hold the battered ribs of Noah's ark, and in the mountain's centre simmers a molten heart that will one day explode. I'd structured my trip so Mt Ararat would be the last place. At night I dreamed about it, sometimes imagined I saw it on the horizon. Yet each morning pulling my body out of bed was like dragging an anvil up from the bottom of the ocean. I could only hobble to the beach and was not well enough for any bus trip. I was disappointed with this body that had once been my friend but was becoming such a nuisance to cart around.

If I could escape through my nostrils at night, flee through the hotel window, cross plains to the mountainside leading up to the galaxy ...

Two months earlier, I'd felt alert and able-bodied as I wandered through the bazaars of Istanbul. Unending streams of people in head veils, *sapkas*, and baseball caps flowed past walls of mounted, kaleidoscope-patterned rugs and gleaming pyramids of dripping mangoes and kumquats; square stacks of neon gelatin cubes coated in sugar stood beside mountains of mismatched sandals and hanging posters of Madonna, Frank Sinatra and the Ayatollah Khomeini. There, in an air smelling of damp brick, cattle excrement and frying garlic, I met Selami. He was a man embarrassed by his name. 'I know in English it means "Italian sausage" but in Turkish it means "charity".'

Did I know of any good hotels with rooms available? I pointed up to mine, the Itska Lodge.

'Can you show me it?' he asked.

In an alleyway, the shout of 'Baklava, one thousand lire' and the screeching of caged chickens were all obliterated beneath an ululating wail. A grey turreted tower stood ringed with loudspeakers.

Selami pointed. 'For Muslims. You are Christian?' He made a sign of the cross with one finger.

At the hotel, only one vacant bed in a room that happened to be mine. Selami's forehead creased. 'Is it OK?'

'Fine.' He was cheerful, friendly and I'd just arrived in Turkey and wanted to meet new people.

He said, 'It will be quite an experience for me, rooming with an American boy.'

Lunch. Glistening roasted mutton on steaming rice, chopped vegetables that looked shellacked.

'There's an Arabic place in the Bronx that has stuff like this,' I said.

Selami and I ate on outdoor stools as men clutching beads and miniature Korans passed.

'I'm not really Muslim,' Selami explained. 'My father taught me how to do all that bowing but I don't like it. Of course in your country, everything's different. Men and women can even kiss on the street.'

'Yeah. I guess there's more open talk of sex and stuff.' I stopped. I asked if he was offended.

He was offended that I'd think him so conservative. 'A lot of Western girls come here for sex with us.'

'What?'

'Girls that are white want us cause we're dark. Most Americans, all Europeans. We call them pawn-girls.'

When I said that wasn't quite true, he laughed as if I simply didn't understand the power of Turkish men.

I told him I'd had a girlfriend in New York but we broke up. It was all so ugly I decided to go as far away on the Earth's surface as possible. 'Thailand would've been farther but I didn't have the flight money.' I explained I'd saved up by working at an office-supply plant, carting around barrels of ink and toner. 'I'm trained to be an accountant – my dad pressured me into it and I kept going for these dress-up job interviews, but I dunno … I guess I didn't want that. Not yet. Probably later. I liked my job though, getting a day's earnings by the sweat of my brow. I'm good at lifting things.' I chewed at a chunk of lamb. 'You know, my ex has no idea I'm here. She'll think I've been kidnapped.'

Selami just shrugged. He said that he was in Istanbul to persuade his uncle, a government official, to exempt him from military service. 'I know it's not fair that I not do it but I don't want to spend two years in the army.'

In the late afternoon we went back to our hotel and lay relaxing on our beds.

'Do you like your new room?'

'I like my new friend,' he said.

At bedtime an awkward moment. The Middle East. Bodies hidden in fabric. Even men keep arms, chests and legs covered. Social interaction is like putting your mouth against a hole in a wall and saying 'who are you' to someone unseen on the other side. But now I was face to face with a near-stranger. If I drop my pants, will it trau-matize him? My back to him, I undid my belt. The next morning I noticed him changing under the covers, so I took my cue and did the same.

The two women were named Nihal and Ottet. We strolled the banks of the stream of orange rinds and excrement. Together we crossed a field of sparse weeds resembling bent, frazzle-tipped electric wires. Their village was four parallel dust-filled streets of flat-roofed brick houses. That they'd boldly invited me, a male Westerner, to accom-pany them astonished me. I studied Nihal's bare forearms. She's allowed to be immodestly dressed because a beach is nearby. And I'm permitted to walk with her because Western men aren't really considered men.

Nihal glanced back tentatively. The surface of my skin felt warm.

A gaggle of women stood by the lone fruit stand and, as in much of Eastern Turkey, they were completely veiled. Two women passed draped in black.

I think the covering of the body draws attention to it. Brief glimpses of exposed skin, a finger curved around a purse-handle, toes peeking from beneath a sandal strap seem lit-up, garishly self-important. I often found myself fixating with microscopic intensity on a slight bone protruding from the side of a wrist, the flash of exposed heel-flesh. The minuscule expanded, filled my brain and at night I dreamed of hands the size of mountains, gigantic toes descending from the sky, and my own body so carefully concealed beneath loose cotton shirts and baggy Kurdish trousers with a draw-string waist, ballooned outward beneath me, became as massive and far-reaching as the Anatolian plains.

At one time, like everyone else I pared my fingernails and cleaned out the secret space between toes, but spirit-like I drifted in and out of rooms without being noticed. Yet here in Turkey my body had moral weight. Take off your shirt in the marketplace and there are cries of outrage; drop your drawers and you'll topple an empire.

The outside world is an eye. This is what some people feel all the time. This is what women feel all the time. I remembered how my girlfriend stared unblinking at the ceiling as I ran my hand along her bare stomach. Women passed me in purdah, even their eyes hidden behind black fabric, walking pieces of night drifting about wind-torn streets. I always kept checking to make sure my sweatshirt zipper was pulled to the top.

Nihal, Ottet and I sat on a log behind her house. Leaning back Nihal slid her fingers through her red-brown hair and I noticed sweat-stains on her T-shirt's armpits.

'This is where I live,' she said, sighing. Her brown eyes looked directly into mine. There was no white in her eyes, just dark. I turned away. She kept staring.

With the patriarch dead, are the daughters at last free?

Somewhere, Arab pop music, but shrunken, contained, a mosquito whining in a box.

We talked of Turkey, the beautiful countryside, the friendly people, and nearby Russia is so cold, Van so dreary, but everybody loves Istanbul. Nihal interspersed comments about her father. He died in a bus crash on the road to Trabzon and his body was never recovered. The authorities were only interested in digging out the European tourists who'd been on board.

Occasionally Nihal pouted, said, 'A very good man,' then would dramatically whisk one hand through her hair, glance at me and sigh. She told me she worked as a secretary in Izmir, would be in Van for only a week. In Izmir she had few friends as she couldn't meet people for she worked constantly.

I told Nihal I was rarely sickly like this. At university each year they chose me for the Rangers Football Team. 'I was known for my twenty-yard dash.'

Finally Ottet stood up and said 'Goodbye.' Walking away she looked back and held Nihal's gaze for a long moment. She disappeared around a brick wall, leaving us completely alone.

I could smell Nihal's hair, sweet like apples. She was looking away but her body seemed to be leaning towards me. Her tan neck skin sloped under a silver chain, her collar bone made a slight dint in her orange cotton T-shirt, her breasts barely visible.

You're a pervert, I thought, she's in mourning.

She sighed more than seemed necessary. 'A very good man.'

She stood up and, for no apparent reason, reached to touch a tree branch above us. Then she sat down closer to me. Her knee was a finger-width away from my right hand, which rested on my thigh. I could easily point my index-finger up like an insect antenna, turn it and touch her. It'd look like an accident. I gazed at my finger, willed it not to do it.

Suddenly in my stomach, the fist opening and closing.

Finally a bell rang in the distance and Nihal slowly stood, eyes lowered. 'I must pray all evening. But we can meet tomorrow again. In the morning at the beach?'

The collar of her T-shirt was dark with sweat.

Of course I would come. I walked home carefully. My legs carried my torso as if it were a carton of eggs that would break if I shook it too much.

At dusk Turkish streets have more shadow than light. People stand, trapped, unmoving figures on a never-changing chessboard.

Each evening, heads down, men would herd together and roam the womanless streets. They milled outside movie theatres, threw lit cigarette stubs to the ground. Every man I met asked me what I thought of Turkish women, then would kick at embedded stones in the pavement.

At the Turkish bath in Ankara the attendant had said, 'This is a modesty wrap.' He flicked the plaid towel twice in the air. 'It must not be removed.' The Turkish men wore them around the waist snugly, folded twice at the top. I tried but could only tie the corners together in a sailor's knot I'd learned in Boy Scouts. I stepped carefully down slippery, echo-filled, tiled corridors. Never had I felt so exposed. The place was nearly empty and the rows of pillars and huge domed ceiling made me feel like I'd accidentally wandered half-naked into a cathedral. I resented this other-culture intrusion in my mind. Opaque, ceiling-high windows gleamed in stone walls and the vertical cement cylinders with running water looked suspiciously like baptismal fonts. I kept thinking I'd round a corner to suddenly stand before an awe-struck congregation holding communion wafers in their mouths. The priest would slowly turn toward me, my sailor's knot unravelling.

'I don't want to meet my uncle but I must. Will you accompany me to Beyoglu?'

'Only if the ship doesn't sink.'

So I followed Selami onto the ferry that goes from West to East Istanbul, crossing the imaginary line that separates Europe from Asia.

Selami stood on deck wearing the white dress shirt I'd lent him and the tie we found in the bazaar. Again he asked if he looked OK and I said, 'You should've bought the crocodile-faced tie. You'd really make an impression.'

And then suddenly – smell of salt water, seagulls screeching overhead, the deck bobbing in the middle of the strait, on both sides of us hills of stacked rectangular buildings with jutting poles, wires, satellite dishes; KODAK, IBM signs flashed, abrupt high-rises thrust skyward; on hill summits, squat domed mosques, their pointy-tipped towers like rockets ready for takeoff – it seemed the world had been ripped in two and we stood in the centre. Everything there was to have could be touched with your fingertips.

It was then I told Selami about Mt Ararat. 'It's the end of my trip and the end of everything. Only one road goes there and it's the one I'm taking.' The bus will climb halfway into the clouds and I'll step out, run-bolt-hurtle straight up its slopes, past forests, lakes, up mile-high glaciers, leave Earth, finally pierce the sun and explode. I'll never be troubled by plantar warts, torn muscles, diarrhoea or whooping cough ever again. It's so much simpler to just not have a body.

What would I be then? Air? Light? Wind? Or something else?

My raised arms were touching the bottom of the hanging

lifeboat. Selami said to lower them because people could see my armpit hair. Later, on the bus I crossed my legs and Selami said my foot sole was too visible.

'But I'm bending it down.'

'Not enough.'

My body was becoming divided into little subunits, each assigned its own value.

Finally I made a huge mistake.

When he said, 'You're not waiting for me at the port; there are a lot of bad people there,' I snapped, 'Selami, I'm not a child. I can take care of myself!'

My guidebook: 'In Turkey anger is only rarely expressed in a direct fashion, especially among friends.'

Selami said, 'Things are no longer good between us. I can feel it.'

Every day with Nihal, my skin burned as she leaned back and ran her fingers through her hair. She repeatedly looked me in the eye, and her hand always seemed to be a hair-breadth away from mine. I wondered what I was doing there.

'The grease on that spinning kebab spit smells like candlewax,' I muttered numbly.

At night I thought of Mt Ararat, closed my eyes and willed my body to heal itself.

On our second last day Nihal surprised me. Her voice became level, free of its characteristic pregnant pauses and vague trailings-off. She said, 'It has been nice to know you. Some day I will marry a Turkish man and have children. I will give you my address. My sisters and I will be happy to receive postcards.' She smiled and her smile was actually very sweet.

'I am happy to hear that.' For that moment I believed her.

Below us the lake glistened.

Someday I will swim in the Lake of Van. Streams of glimmering suds will rush round my body and I will be cleansed, simplified, made pure.

* * *

'If I lived in the West, I wouldn't be lazy like you,' said Selami. I'd started to pretend not to hear him. 'I bet you I could immigrate there, no problem. The officials would love me.'

I became exasperated whenever he refused to go into a restaurant not displaying Pepsi signs. He talked of McDonald's the way I talked of Mt Ararat.

Then all at once everything changed. Perhaps we became tired of bickering. On a park bench by the Bosphorus, he started to run his fingers through my hair. In Turkey it's socially acceptable for men to show affection for each other; you see them walking hand in hand all the time. Selami asked me to put my head in his lap. 'But are your legs sweating?' I asked.

The folds of his cotton khaki pants felt soft against the back of my head; beneath were his hard, thin thighs. He stroked my cheeks, jawline.

He spoke sadly. 'I think I will probably live all my life in Izmir. After the military I will be a tobacco exporter like my father. You can come visit me.'

'That would be nice.'

'Yes,' said Selami. And with that he looked up and out over the water.

My last day in Van, I awoke, took a deep breath and noticed my body didn't shiver. I removed an article of clothing. Again I thought of my father who often said, 'Don't show anyone your weak side or they'll never stop baiting you.'

As I waited at the beach, a squat carbuncled man in his underwear ran up, 'Come, come,' he cried, his hand beat in my face like a bird's little wing. I always follow those who beckon. But the man's pushiness was irritating.

Still, I let myself be pulled along and followed him up the beige stone outcropping that swells up from the beach, a series of irregular steps full of pocky holes and protruding globules, as if the entire mount were once molten rock that had bubbled and popped in the sun, then solidified. In the top a crater opening into a sheltered cove and below, the water. The sun beamed down; here everything was lit up.

I sat on a lopsided ledge, peeked over the crater lip, saw the whole beach. The little man sat opposite, smiling back. Sparse black hairs made diagonal stripes on his bulbous forehead and like all Turkish men, he had a moustache. Peculiar, red, wart-like growths sprouted on his chest and arms.

'I live Van,' he said. 'And you?'

'Manhattan.'

'Ah yes, yes,' and then, 'you *guzel*.' I'd always used this word when people asked my opinion of Turkey. It meant 'beautiful'. I shifted on the bumpy ledge that instantly felt uncomfortable.

He stared at my bare forearms and I wished I'd kept my sweater on. I looked at my skin, disturbingly white and bright as if lit up within by thousand tiny light bulbs I couldn't turn off.

I picked up a stone and flung it towards the lake.

'Ah!' said the man, his eyes followed its trajectory. '*Kulte, kulte,*' he said. '*Kulte.*' He wanted me to repeat it.

'*Kulte*,' I said politely.

Kulte was Turkish for 'stone'.

He touched a patch of dirt in a hole. '*Hosi.*'

'*Hosi.*'

He pointed and moved his finger and said, '*Parmak.*' Turkish for 'finger'?

'*Parmak.*'

I relaxed. He taught me 'eye', 'nose', 'mouth', 'chin'. I repeated the parts of his body to him. 'Elbow,' 'chest' and finally he said '*kamis*', Turkish for penis and pulled his out.

I sat stunned. This was the first sexual organ I'd seen in Turkey. Evidently he did not believe in modesty wraps. With two fingers he made scissor-like motions at its head, implying, I suppose, he was circumcised. 'And you?'

I pretended not to understand.

Again he repeated, '*kamis*'. He gestured; he wanted to see mine.

I felt like a fool. Should I have realized this was going on when he asked me up here? I felt the protective weight of my double-knit shirt, my heavy wool pants on my still-weak body. I said, 'No thank you, I've had food poisoning.'

He stared, completely still. Had he understood? He pointed once at my trousers and said firmly, 'Yes. Yes.'

Turning my head I saw, below on the beach, Nihal running along the edge of the water.

'Well, it's time for me to go.' I stood up.

'Go?' he said. 'Go?' Then, 'Not go!' He began motioning furiously towards his swollen penis and pointing at my hand. I pretended not to notice what was happening.

'It was nice meeting you,' I said. I reached forward to shake his hand and when his sweating fingers pressed into mine, his whole body convulsed and started trembling.

I'd read homosexuality was illegal in Eastern Turkey, punishable by one hundred lashes or death, whichever came first. This man had probably never left Van, was surely married, maybe had never been with a man but had waited for one. On the beach he sees a rare Westerner who would surely disappear the next day and not say a word to anyone, a white man from a permissive land where people will do anything. His only chance?

I looked into his creasing face, gaping agony-flecked eyes; need emanated from him like heat. 'I'm sorry,' I said. 'I'm sorry.' His hand still urgently grasped mine, his penis glowed poker-red; he could hardly speak.

My body remained inert as the static rocks round me and I had not the desire to leap through the space between us. For the first time in months I did not feel split into parts and when I glanced at my freckled forearms, realized my skin surrounded me on all sides and was more impermeable than it seemed. I couldn't leap out of it if I tried. Sweat drops snaked along my hairline and I felt myself sinking down warmly into my torso and spreading out like tentacles into the far extremities of my fingers and toes. How cosy to be nestled like a chick in an egg and wrapped round with the spiral umbilical of my bloodstream. I'll never attempt to go beyond the edges of my skin ever again.

I abruptly jerked my hand from the man's, stepped back, turned and, as I neared the top of the ridge, heard his choked cry.

And so I left him the man there, one hand outstretched, his body shaking, an embodiment of pure, untrammelled, exposed desire on the edge of the clear, faultless waters of Lake Van and in my imagination he stands there still.

As I ran down the stone hill, I felt I was Zeus swooping down from the sky to Nihal who crouched extracting a rock from the earth. Waves beat on the gravel shore. I felt strong and full of a strange courage.

'Nihal,' I said happily. 'I'm going to Mt Ararat tomorrow. I'm positive I can go there.' And when I looked up, I was sure I could see its peaks in the distance. Its perfectly straight, glacier-frozen tip touched the sky.

'Thanks for speaking to me the first day in the bazaar,' I said to Selami. 'It has been a fun time.'

Selami said it's a Turkish custom that when two friends part, they exchange an article of clothing so whenever they wear them, they think of the other person. He wanted the shirt I was wearing. 'I like the collar; it's so American.'

I removed my shirt and gave it to him.

When we said goodbye, we did the Muslim kiss. Of course I did it wrong. The lips are just supposed to graze the side of the cheek but I turned and pressed mine right into his hot skin.

When I said goodbye to Nihal, I made sure my sweatshirt zipper was done up. Already she had left me and had the unfocused gaze she got in the late afternoon, re-entering her fog of mourning.

We both half-smiled and said goodbye at the same time.

Then I turned and jumped over the river of excrement. Halfway across, a flash of panic as I thought I was falling, but my foot touched a hard, concrete bank and I made it. Just barely.

Earthquakes on the Far Side of the World

I remember the gentle rise of your stone-solid chest, its scattered hairs bending like windblown grasses.

But you are far away now, Franz, and I've returned to my basement, a place you've never been, that perhaps you never imagined, an eight-metre square carved in the ground beneath a five-storey rectangle. There are no pictures on my walls but I have two chairs, a bed, microscope, stacked plastic cubes containing rock samples, and a computer whose screen is as dark as a moonless night sky. When I sleep, my hand twitches in empty space on the bedspread as, with my ear pressed to a pillow pressed to a futon pressed to the earth I hear, from 12,753 kilometres below, the fire burning at the Earth's centre. There, lava continually coagulates into gigantic globules that collapse downward into a sea of fire, then break apart and flow up to join other steaming, shifting masses in a subterranean landscape that perpetually devours and recreates itself amidst an eternal sulphur spray, the deafening roar of conflagrating carbon and a constant temperature of 3,700 degrees Celsius.

In the morning when I wake, you are everywhere. Your shoulder is the rock sheath jutting from the sand beside the parking lot. Distant granite cliffs are the edge of your forehead and nose. Stone spheres protruding from the ground are the nodules in your spine. With hands on ears I run down long, cement-walled streets, through car-flurried intersections, across deserted squares, over empty, windwhipped fields, but no matter how fast I run, no matter how far I go, there is always the sudden, scuffled scrape of unearthed stone beneath my feet and the sound of the fire roaring at the Earth's centre.

You are everywhere, Franz.

But then again, you are nowhere.

I have stood on the edges of oceans straining to see your face in the horizon. I have shouted your name into windstorms, waved huge placards from atop mountain cliffs, but the world is too vast, Franz, distances are too great and the Atlantic Ocean is like a wall between us.

Franz lives right round the other side of the world in a placid city in a valley where snow rarely falls, and instead, piles of money stand along the streets, ring the city, sometimes arching so high you can't see over them and citizens have long, involved discussions about whether the outside world has really ceased to exist. Tramcars continually travel up one street and down another, as tourist guides talk of cheese and watches because they don't know what else to say, and each cobbled stone in every quiet lane is polished daily with a toothbrush, people are outraged when candy boxes arrive with some chocolates upside down and some right side up, and Parliament is convened and a national emergency declared when a lone drop of precipitation is seen falling from the sky.

I have nightmares, Franz. I have nightmares about the polar ice caps melting, that you in your silent valley will vanish beneath the spreading surface of a saltwater sea. Or perhaps it will be simpler. You will fall beneath the scissor-sharp wheels of the tramcars you love and then be tossed like a rock into the waters of Zurichsee. The bankers won't care but will examine the ripples on the surface, and, making sure their briefcases are locked, pull their neckties even tighter.

What would happen if Franz vanished? Would the wind stop blowing, the sky stop changing as it does from puce to turquoise to ochre? Would the Earth become an ice cube that suddenly cracks?

Franz, though I know you have long forgotten me, though my name is just a sound half heard in the wind, a fragment of a syllable in a language you no longer understand, I have sent you letters full of the sentences that confine my life, but the planes carrying them were shot down by pellet-eyed terrorists, and my scraps of paper scattered across all the oceans of this world to wash up on distant, wave-ravaged shores or be swallowed by razor-fanged fish.

Only one letter reached you.

Could you understand its hieroglyphics or did it dissolve like a snowflake in your hands?

Zurich is a hiding-place in a moderate climate where the temperature sometimes hovers around zero and has never plunged since that fateful day years ago – centuries ago it seems – when I flew across the ocean carrying my suitcase full of rocks.

I should've known something would happen. I should've calculated the angle Zurich makes to Toronto using the Earth's centre as the vertex, but back then I only studied the surface of things, and from my city to Zurich was a 6,500-kilometre straight line, meaningless as a dangling thread.

I sat at a table before a crowd of what I assumed were mostly scientists. In my bag were gleaming cobalt, latticed obsidian, half mineral, part sandstone trachyte, pock-cratered felsite. To one side the podium and the German doctor speaking. My knees shook slightly. I was not used to crowds, not comfortable with public speaking, though I'd made myself take a course in it once. I remembered to breathe deeply in and out, concentrating, as I'd been told, on the air passing through one nostril.

Then, applause.

It was my turn. I stood up.

The auditorium was a dark, shifting sea before which I held bits of rock I'd gathered from the surface of my country. 'The basalt of northern Ontario has a magnesium content of 10 to 16 weight-percent ... the lines on such devonian rock have coalesced from separate microcratons or microplates over a very long period of time.'

As I turned the rocks in my hands, my fingertips pressed their contours, their jagged crevices, bubble-lipped craters, crystals shimmered, sending off bits of reflected light that danced in the surrounding air.

Still, before me, the dark mass throbbing like a huge, restless amoeba.

When the lights came up for questions, all the people in chairs were scattered willy-nilly across the floor's great surface. The shadowed, outer edges of the crowd pressed against walls that pushed inwards, and the sea of people flowed backwards against the room's rear wall, out the back doors and into the half-lit corridor. Arms flew up like sticks rising from a flooded swamp.

As I answered questions, I began to notice Franz. He was sitting in the front centre of the room, as still as a boulder, or a cliff standing over the ocean.

Afterwards he approached me grinning. His eyes slitted. It seemed he was perpetually winking. 'Have you thought of bringing stones engraved with sentences from your speeches and distributing them in kits to people who arrive for your lectures?'

'Of course not,' I said, annoyed. 'How could people take such rocks home? They'd rip the seams of any shopping bags you put them in.'

'The people don't have to use shopping bags. They could use potato sacks, wheelbarrows, or if they're from your country, sleds equipped with dog teams. Besides, not all shopping bags break.'

'I know nothing about shopping bags.' I realized for the first time that I'd never thought deeply about them before. 'I have never done study on shopping-bag seams. But I suppose I could.'

'It might be a good idea.' Franz smiled at me and his eyes slitted again.

Behind, a line of people in lab coats stood waiting to talk to me.

I asked, 'What is your field exactly, sir?'

'I'm not a scientist. I'm an artist doing a rock installation. I once loved air, wind and windmills but rock is the most solid thing there is. It's what we stand on, right?'

'We stand on rock but rock stands on fire.'

Franz's mouth twisted and he raised one eyebrow. His tongue quickly passed over lips that were full and wet. His forehead and jaw were square; his whole head looked like a mailbox standing on one side.

He picked up a pebble from the display table. 'So this is a rock from your country.' He looked straight at me. There was a knife-blade flash in his eyes. 'Amazing. That I can hold something native to a place that's so far away and so vast.' His gaze fixated on it. 'Really quite something.' He rotated the rock. 'It doesn't reflect any light though.'

'It contains no quartz crystal. Quartz catches light.'

He stared into its surface. 'Is it dangerous?' he joked.

'Dangerous?'

'Would this rock harm me?'

Not able to make witty repartee, I just said, 'No.'

Then the man squeezed the rock between his two fingers, his eyes flamed, he popped it into his mouth and, to my amazement and horror, swallowed. His Adam's apple bulged briefly forward, then receded to its former position.

I gasped. 'You just swallowed a trabylite rock!'

'So?'

'It'll rupture your oesophagus, or shred your stomach muscles! It could kill you!'

'You told me it wasn't dangerous.'

'I didn't think you'd try to eat it.'

'But such rocks have a tantalizing look.'

'No, they don't!' I cried. 'I've gathered thousands of such rocks and have never had the desire to eat one.'

'You should be aware of cultural differences. To Europeans, all things Canadian are harmless and innocent.'

I turned away. 'My God.' I put my face in my hands. I felt responsible. 'A bit of Ontario just went down your gullet. I'm sorry,' I cried, 'I never knew rocks were that tempting. Ambulance! We need an ambulance!'

I sat beside Franz on the way to the hospital.

'Don't go blaming yourself,' he said. 'You didn't force the rock between my teeth or anything.'

I couldn't think of a word to say.

'And I didn't have to swallow it,' Franz said.

'Still, I'm sorry.'

Suddenly he took my hand in his. The ambulance went over a bump and I heard that little bit of Ontario rattling around in his oesophagus.

At the hospital the x-ray showed that the rock had miraculously dissolved and been absorbed into his bloodstream. Speechless, I stared at the translucent sheet displaying all his inner organs lit up like the iridescent forms of the aurora borealis. The trabylite stone had most likely been broken down in the pancreatic membrane and was now entering the ductile marrow of his bones.

When I put down the sheet, Franz smiled at me from his bed and asked me out for lunch the next day.

I stood still, stunned. I've had flings before. I've spent the night with men who are like breezes that scuttle along the Earth's surface, disturbing not so much as a leaf. I am such a man myself. I give speeches before crowds that forget me. I write articles few people read. I am a man who lives in a basement and looks through a microscope lens and have never asked for anything more.

Yet here was a man whose body had struggled with stone and conquered it.

I said, 'Yes. Let's meet at noon.'

'We can talk about everything. I want to hear about the country you live in. It's a place I've never been.'

The country I live in? I come from a country people rarely visit and which for some hardly exists. What could be said of my home? I suddenly saw myself alone in an empty field, crouched staring at a rock in my hand, as winds blew all about me, but I could not lift my head to see where I lived because, if I did, the precious stone I clutched, its glittering crystals and asymmetrical ridges, would dissolve to dust and vanish in the wind.

I got up the next morning and observed the sun on the lower lip of Zurich's valley. In the mirror the skin on my face looked smooth, unblemished. I fingered the subtle bump of my barely visible cheekbone, the budgie-like beak of my nose. I am not a good-looking man. In Toronto once a month a friend takes me to a disco where I sit in the corner watching men out of the corner of my eye. Otherwise, I play pin-the-tail-on-the-mastodon with an old lady down the hall. In my life there's no largeness of gesture and when someone offers me pleasure, albeit vague and fleeting, I respond, and that satisfies me.

The tram made a high-pitched, humming sound as it slid along its silver rails, moving so smoothly through the cobbled streets I felt I was floating on air. The metal-slat seat vibrated just slightly beneath me. The city was calm that morning. Perhaps Zurich always seems calm. Gleaming, silver-trimmed cars glided soundlessly from one street to the other, boys on shining bicycles seemed to drift in slow motion up the city's small hills, an elderly woman wearing a hat mounted with a stuffed bird carefully sipped her coffee in an empty sidewalk café, as a teenager with safety pins in his cheeks crouched combing his orange rooster-tuft before a shop window. At intersections everything came to a stop as groups of men in identical, square-shouldered, dark suits and women carrying shopping bags draped with bits of lace and floating wisps of gauze walked in single file between parallel lines printed on uncracked pavement. One man's tie blew over his shoulder and he stopped walking to carefully tuck it back in.

When we got to Zurich's little lake, there was not a ripple on its surface, and all the small boats were docked. The whole city appeared to be waking up but, in truth, it was the height of the day.

Little did I know that below the ground, continental plates were shifting, buckling their shoulders hard up against each other, and that steam was building up below the Earth's crust.

At the end of the line, at the end of the road, Franz stood smiling in a red cotton T-shirt and bright turquoise jean jacket.

He beckoned me behind a bush, 'I hope you're hungry,' and there I saw a picnic table covered with paper plates and piles of sliced cheeses and meats and paper cups and thermoses of drinks.

I said, 'You didn't have to do all this!'

'I bring a typical Swiss breakfast cause I'm a typical Swiss guy.' Throwing his head back, he laughed.

And then we sat. And ate.

Thick slices of piquant salami that left grease dripping from our lips, steaming cornbread that smelled so sweet, I had to press it to my nose and inhale before swallowing, acrid olives that singed my tongue and palate, sleek-skinned grapes that exploded between my teeth, sweet-tangy quark that expanded flooding my mouth, and Franz's own private, special concoction 'that I invented one day when it wouldn't stop raining and my fridge was too full' ... yogurt mixed with cranberries and pomegranate seeds and muesli and sliced peaches, pears, passion fruit, pineapple rings, barley rinds and crabapples.

Oh, how we laughed as we ate, not bothering to wipe the food from our faces. We talked of everything, hiking boots, airplane tickets, elevator music, the difficulty of tying sailor's knots, paintings that don't stay on walls, ice cream that's been refrozen, fire extinguishers, and the hard core at the centre of avocados we both always wanted to eat but couldn't.

But the food was not enough and so afterwards we gathered stones, pebbles, and cement chips and put them in our mouths. I hesitated for a moment and swallowed. I felt a pleasant warm trembling in the centre of my body. Franz and I glanced at each other and grinned.

And then he looked me in the eye and said again, 'Your country, Greg. Tell me about your country.'

And again I was in an empty field staring down at a pock-marked rock and, though the wind blew all around me, I dared not lift my head.

I plucked a blade of grass, placed it against my lip.

'Who cares about my country.' I said. 'What about yours?'

Franz leaned back, chuckled. The sun shone just above his head. 'My country,' he said raising both hands, 'this is it.'

And so I followed him. Into the forest and down long, winding, rock-strewn paths, over twisted tree roots that clutched the earth like giant fingers, beneath fungi-webbed branches, beside boulder-studded streams, in and out of cratered, limestone gulleys, through rhyolite-rimmed chasms, past moss-mouthed caves where stalactites have been dripping for the past two thousand years, and when we got to the edge of a granite pit, Franz took his sweater off.

We were both sweating. Dark blotches marked the back of his T-shirt, his armpits, the top of his chest. Above, leaves rustled and light specks danced over his thick thighs, his narrow nose that sloped forward like a ski jump, his low forehead with bangs that, from here, seemed to be unevenly cut. We were both breathing heavily.

Then he turned to me and spoke in a voice as hushed as the sound a breeze makes moving in and out of the portals of underground caverns or passing through the shaded knotholes of felled trees.

'Thanks for coming, stone man.'

'I could've stayed in but didn't. This morning the tramcar shot along its rails like the arrow towards William Tell's apple.'

A shadow trembled on Franz's cheek and he said, 'I spoke to you yesterday because your eyeballs were conflagrating. Were you aware of that? Such a small man you seemed. Are you aware of that too? Throughout your speech your eyes flamed so that the tops of your cheeks appeared to be melting, pouring like wax down your face and dripping onto the podium. Such a contrast between your eyes and your body and your clothes. Like that shirt. Where did you buy it?'

'Wal-Mart.'

'That makes me very sad,' Franz said and his head dropped. 'I have been surrounded by dancing go-go boys all my life. They are all of one and nothing of everything. I have pulled myself from the meat market and thought art could do things. But winds only blow and rock is inert. And then I saw you, someone from a place I've never been and probably will never go. I had to discover who you were. This city is so small. My country is so small. Sometimes it seems I know everyone in it. But you're from a place so huge and far from the centre.' He stepped towards me, 'I think you're very nice,' and quickly and unobtrusively, he kissed me on the lips – I smelled his sweat, his aftershave and a cinnamon-soap scent – he sauntered away and sat on a flat rock protruding from the ground.

I crouched on a stone outcropping that pressed against my behind.

He pulled out a knife and cut an apple. 'Are you still hungry?'

He handed me an apple half. 'We could've got to my place faster but I prefer the scenic route. You may think you're far from Zurich, but in that direction another town begins. You head any direction and you'll soon come to a border, the German, Italian or Austrian. We're surrounded by borders. I often think about going away.' A breeze moaned through the treetops. 'I fantasize about leaving just as that moss bed fantasizes about sprouting daisies, and that tree stump wishes it could grow branches, and that bull thistle dreams of shedding its thorns.'

I didn't say anything. I thought things were normal in my life. I thought I was just fine and nothing was changing. I didn't know that on the far side of the world, earthquakes were happening in the country I lived in, granite mountains were imploding and shale cliffs were falling into the sea.

I lifted the piece of apple he gave me, put it in my mouth. My hand was shaking.

Franz pointed down to the dark cleft in the centre of the pit. 'Fall in that, you'll probably keep on falling and never stop.'

For the first time I heard it, the sound that would follow me for the rest of my life: the fire burning at the Earth's centre. Molten lava separated to join swelling masses that broke apart to meld with others ...

I looked at Franz and he looked at me and our apple cracked between our teeth. A bird flew overhead. Somewhere water trickled. The forest was dark and was light and was dark.

And then Franz took my hand and led me the rest of the way down the twisting trail until we stood on the edge of the clearing where he lived. In the middle was his cabin, triangle-peaked, built of stone brick and mortar, thin-walled but, in this temperate climate, all he needed. And studded throughout the grounds, his artwork, things that would remain in my mind a lifetime: large stone circles with lines through them and clay spheres penetrated by steel rods that went in one side and out the other; everything round was divided yet connected by lines that criss-crossed at multitudinous angles, and everything was chopped into segments that fit into a framework that was spherical – plastic, slatted wheels rotated on metal axles, wooden hoops adorned with streamers whirled round rotating iron poles, as huge metallic discs spun in the wind, their styrene spokes clattering against outthrusting metal prongs. Everything had an axis as well as an outer surface, and I realized if you drew a line from my country to the Earth's centre, it joined a similar line from Switzerland and our two countries were connected in an obvious, logical, not even mysterious way. Immediately I saw myself in my own barren field studying the crystal-flecked surface of a rock that now seemed completely insignificant, and as Franz's words pushed relentlessly against my eardrums, 'Tell me about your country, tell me, tell me ...', I finally let the rock drop to the ground and – I lifted my head and I saw where I lived.

I beheld a vast plain and a forest and beyond, another forest and lakes and cliffs and more forests and trees and plains and rocks, and suddenly a shrieking wind from the Arctic Circle hurtled down across an endless wilderness to blast every cell in the surface, subsurface and core layers of my body.

I'd never seen myself so clearly before.

I said, 'Franz my country, my country is –' and as pronged wheels clattered furiously at the back of my head, I told Franz everything: How the fierce, ravenous, northern winds roar down across seven billion forests full of one thousand billion trees, where it tears off pine branches, fractures birches, uproots junipers and wild crocuses, drags up rocks from the earth, and dashes grey gritty water against cliffs; the air is ever full of the piercing wail of starved coyotes, coyotes and grizzly bears; snow falls in avalanches from the sky, becomes an army of ice-pebbles beating your cheeks, as gazing at empty horizons, you call out for a warm breeze that never comes – for your heart can pound all it wants but your blood will never be enough to warm the extremities of your body, and your thigh muscles can strain all they can but will never hold your torso straight against the storm, and you can turn the furnace of your house to 300 degrees Celsius, barricade your doors behind mile-high mountains of wool blankets, but the wind will smash every window of every building you've ever been in, hurl your wool coverings to the farthest corners of the Earth and drive its steel, icy poles into every pore in your skin at once.

In the country I live in, it is always minus 7,000 degrees Celsius, the wind has never stopped blowing, and winter is a thousand months long.

Seeing Franz before me, I immediately hurled myself onto the inexpressible warmth of his body and, as my mouth wandered wildly over the rock-edge of his chin, the hard, level expanse of his chest, the solid protuberance of his groin, an Arctic wind beat at my back and neck, drove snowflakes through my hair, striking faster, colder as Franz's flesh burned like fire beneath me.

That day for the first time in the history of the world, there was a snowstorm in Switzerland at the height of summer. Shopkeepers gazed up in disbelief as white flakes appeared in what had been a blue sky, and all the bankers stopped walking and looked down to check that the date dials on their watches were correct. Soon tram-cars couldn't run because the streets were clogged, and all the café owners had to take their tables and chairs inside and change the day's special from pasta salad to fondue.

When Franz and I finished making love, we looked out at a world transformed into an endless series of ghost-like mounds of pure white snow.

It is rare that one does not jar in some way with the environment where one finds oneself. The world is 4.6 billion years old and the subterranean plates of its continents have shifted and readjusted themselves many times. The Earth is so altered from what it once was (if we can ever with certainty know that) and has become so complex and multifarious that it's nearly impossible to find an organism completely aligned with every element in its habitat. But that's the way I seemed to be during the following weeks in Zurich.

I am sure you remember, Franz. Though your country has closed its borders to me and the café awnings are all folded up and the bankers' briefcases locked tighter than ever, I'm sure there are moments when you see my face in a flash of light reflected in a shopwindow or in the blurred flutter of wings as pigeons fly from the fountain beside Alfred Escher's statue, and that at times, in darkest night, when your city is engulfed in its tomb-like silence, you can hear the faint, barely perceptible sound of me weeping on the far side of the world.

I know you'd never forget how wonderful things were for us. How we wandered arm in arm down the streets of the city you lived in, as snowbanks rose on all sides of us, growing higher and higher, glittering beneath a brittle crystal sun in a subzero cold I could no longer feel. I forgot calendars existed, Franz. I was deaf to the sound of the Swiss timepieces ticking in the windows of every shop we passed, on the wall of every restaurant we ate in, on the wrist of everyone who stared at us in the street.

The silent snow, the undulating rise and fall of its knolls and dales, was all to me, the laughing children throwing snowballs across the street, the teenagers skating in circles on the frozen lake, the water dripping down the steam-covered insides of café windows, the icicles that hung like gleaming, metallic spears everyone feared would drop. And that day I made a magnificent, life-sized snowman of you right there in the middle of the financial district and it lasted two days before a plough came and took it away.

I could press handfuls of snow against my cheeks and feel no pain, could hold fingers of ice to my teeth and feel no sorrow, and when I touched the nylon surface of your winter coat, though it seemed as thick as the internal layers of the Earth, I could feel your heart beating deep inside you. And how I came to know your body in that short time, its hillocks and glens, stone ridges and hidden valleys. I knew it as I once knew the houses on the street I lived on, the walls of my basement apartment, my trays full of rocks and my night-black computer screen.

I think you enjoyed those days, Franz.

How you'd laugh before the fireplace when we rolled about on your rug. How glorious you looked feasting in that Italian restaurant, your hands full of bread, lips moist from tomato sauce, your face beaming above the bright-white, rippling napkin wrapped round your neck. You chattered so sillily in that cinema where we saw the terrible movie about the jewellery thieves stranded in the Sahara desert, and you were serious too, Franz. Do you remember when you told me about your father's death, you were so young and it so unexpected, and how you'd always wanted to be a deep-sea diver but have ended up living your life here, in Switzerland, the most land-locked country in the world. You would press your face into my shoulder and let me stroke your hair as I talked of wind-swept glaciers, flowers that bloom once a century in the sun-starved tundra and the vast outer reaches of the Arctic Ocean covered with ice that will never melt. I think you enjoyed those weeks, Franz. I think you were happy with me then. I see no reason to think otherwise.

But some days you would not look me in the eye and said little as the shadows of your valley deepened into the blackness of night. Was it the ticking of the clocks?

I sometimes even wondered if your and my countries were all that different, Franz. It disturbed me to think I was with someone who in some ways was me. I should've fallen for a Latino or an Italian whose arms move in the air like streamers in the wind, not a man who neatly tucks his shirt in before nodding at the cashier at Credit Suisse. Europe has made me ridiculous. Shouldn't I want the pure opposite of me?

Finally one morning my finger grazed the edge of the airplane ticket I'd left in my suitcase pocket, and I realized that the snow-banks and sunlit sheets of ice and your mouth swiftly pressing against mine on the street when I turned to say, 'Which way is south, Franz? Which way is north?' – all would vanish as snow becomes slush, becomes water that disappears into the ground.

But still I couldn't accept this.

That afternoon I went to the Swiss authorities. I had already been questioned once, as had all the conference invitees for surely there had been some link between their arrival and the destruction of the Swiss summer tourist season. Everyone blamed the Iraqis, but some thought Russia was at fault, and many believed an American woman who'd said the Pentagon's five-point design wasn't aesthetically pleasing was the culprit. Of course I wasn't suspected and my interrogation had been a formality. I come from a country people never visit and that most don't believe exists.

I knocked politely on the door marked Switzerland Immigration, entered and took out my passport.

A man sat at a wide, wooden desk where he was stamping small strips of paper. Behind him sat similar people at similar desks with similar paper strips.

'Hello,' I said.

'*Guten Tag*,' he replied.

The man had pointed, diagonal streaks of grey in his jet-black hair and he wore rectangular, iron-framed glasses whose thick lenses made his eyes small, pinched and crab-like.

I sat on the steel-backed chair in front of him.

In mid-stamp he looked back at me and said, 'Yes?'

I cleared my throat. 'I want to stay here,' I said softly. 'For a little while. Or maybe a few years.' I added, 'Or perhaps for the rest of my life.'

He glared at me, set aside his metal stamp. His thin-lipped mouth didn't smile.

'Because,' I said, my head down, 'I think it will be good for me.'

The man said something abruptly in German and handed me a form in four languages, none of them English.

I followed the French instructions as best I could and eventually handed him back the sheet with pieces missing, boxes not checked off and lines left blank.

'I'm sorry,' I said. 'I can't understand these languages well.'

The man's right eyebrow peaked. He said in English, 'I see.' With lips pursed, he looked over what little I'd written. Then he took my passport and flipped through it peremptorily. He said, 'And what do you propose to do in Switzerland? What abilities do you have for us?'

'I ... I can look at rocks. I'm a geologist. I can look at a rock and determine its chemical content.' He stared back unmoving. 'You see,

I need to be here. I think it will be good for me.'

'You think it will be good for you?'

'Yes.'

One of his eyelids quivered. 'You cannot speak any of our official languages and have a completely irrelevant skill.' He coughed once. 'I'm sorry, Mr –' he glanced at the sheet, 'Johnson. We do not give out residence or work permits for such spontaneous demands unless there is an urgent reason involved. And I must tell you that you have little to offer our country employment-wise. We have no need for rock-examiners in Switzerland. Our economy is not defined by pieces of rock but by money. Money,' he repeated, 'made of paper, resin and ink.' He reached into his pocket, let drop a handful of bills that wafted across the table. 'If our banks were full of rocks, you could spend your time counting them. But as it is, you will find no rocks in any of our banks here. Of course there are many rocks in the Swiss countryside but we prefer to leave them unexamined.'

'But you see,' I said, gulping, I'd tell him everything, 'I like somebody. And he's of the male sex so I can't legally marry and stay here. But if I were here, I could help him with his sundials and oil the spinning, plastic wheels every morning and push metal sticks into clay globes so they're perfectly perpendicular to the axes.' I said shyly, 'I think it will be good for him ... for me ... for us.'

Just then the man and all the people listening at the desks behind burst into loud, raucous laughter. They shouted things back and forth in a language I couldn't understand.

Wiping his eyes and putting his glasses back on, the man said, 'Switzerland has a great love of the homosexual people. We would never put you in camps or force you to walk down the street wearing funny hats. But such unions have no legal status. They have no effect on the speed of our tramways or the quality of nuts in our chocolate or the price of gold bullion. They do –' he snatched the bills from the table, stuffed them back in his pocket, 'nothing for us. So Mr Johnson, I'm sorry,' and he stamped – BANG – a black square in my passport, 'you must leave before the date stated.' He handed me my blue leather booklet labelled with the name of my country on the outer edge of the Earth and said, 'Bon voyage.'

Outside it'd stopped snowing. A cold wind pierced the fabric of my thin, rayon coat. I stared into the frozen waters of Zurichsee and said, 'I thought it would be good for me. I thought it would be good.'

Franz was asleep beneath his comforter when I arrived and when he awoke, rose and prepared himself a hot chocolate. He sat bleary-eyed, his hair tousled, as his lips tentatively sipped at the steaming liquid.

I said abruptly, 'Franz, I have to leave tomorrow. There's no legal way I can stay on. I tried, but –'

'Let be,' he said angrily. 'Let be.'

What were you thinking when you said that, Franz? Let be. I have spent a lifetime examining these words. I have studied the form of their letters under a microscope. I have made clay figures of them that I beat into dust and sifted through for some hint of their compositional qualities. I have played tapes of those two simple, one-syllable words over and over, searching for what connection they have to the sound of plates shifting beneath the Earth's crust and the hiss of steam stealing through underground caves.

The night before I left Zurich, as I lay awake in the dark beside Franz, I could hear the sound of the Earth creaking on its axis. It is an old world we live on, Franz. It has spun round so many times, I'm often amazed its central shaft hasn't rusted and cracked causing our whirling globe to finally come to a halt. We are not the first to touch its surface with our hands. We are not the first who have pressed its glimmering rocks against our skin. The snow has fallen so many times before and then frozen, and melted, then frozen again. There is so much, Franz, that we can never know. There are layers of stone from the Precambrian era concealed beneath rock from the Phanerozoic period and below there are strata, seams and lamina from epochs we know nothing of, that we do not yet have names for, that may never be discovered. In our lifetimes, Franz, we can only know such a small portion of what exists. The world is endless, Franz, and its treasures are inexhaustible.

Even if we could penetrate the Earth's hard skin and journey deep towards its fiery heart, the now-buried diorite and glittering amethyst, the purple-bubbled gabbro-rock and streaked pegmatite would soon completely surround us and ignite in us a wonder that would hold you and me stationary between the surface and the centre as the Earth spins slowly, so slowly that those who have always lived on its outer rim think the world is motionless and that the sky is moving.

As morning light began to flow around the edges of your window blind, I had the sudden desire to clutch your body against mine. But I was afraid to wake you. Somehow I thought you'd be furious. At what? At my impracticality? Or at how geography rules us? That I'd stayed too long? Or too little? Let be. The words an indecipherable tattoo forever beating in my brain. Let be, let be, let be.

And then what happened, Franz?

After the breakfast of chopped salami from which oil wouldn't drip but had congealed into a paste on each slice, cornbread whose crust was now so hard we couldn't get a knife through it, and mango juice that had gone rancid and left canker sores in our mouths, we headed out into a world where everything had speeded up. The Earth spun in reverse as we went up twisting, rock-strewn trails, through moss-rimmed craters, stepped in and out of mud footprints that would, from now on, point in one direction only, past open-mouthed caves where stalactites had finally stopped dripping, and then the empty tram stop, and the tramcar hurtling through the shadow-striped streets lined with snowbanks I saw even now were starting to melt, and then what happened at the airport? Who put all those tunnels there?

We were lost in an endless, underground labyrinth where we turned right and left and then back and around, following arrows that pointed up, down, in all directions at once, and then forwards and backwards, forever trapped in unending, barely lit, winding, stone-walled corridors, and then suddenly we were out on the tarmac, the wind blowing my hair as my scarf lashed from my neck like a wild thing trying to be free, and you looked at me (his body conquered stone) and I looked down at my flapping ticket (a country no one visits) and I lifted my head (as I lifted my head, my rock dropped to the earth), you said my name and then your voice fissured.

'It has been a wonderful time. I will always remember. Please do not write me. We live too far apart and it's not practical. I think it's best we forget and move on,' and he turned and headed into the tunnel entrance and when the door closed on his shale-slate, stone-spined back forever, I wondered: what will become of my country now?

I turned and saw ten iron steps leading into the aircraft. I thought that climbing those stairs would be the hardest thing I'd ever have to do. When I tore my foot from the earth and let it bang down on the first step, a huge crevice formed in the Northwest Territories and spread south all the way through Manitoba, thus permanently separating East from West. As my left foot struck the second stair, the Continental Divide cracked and British Columbia was thrown into the ocean, never to be seen again. The third step, the Maritimes were consumed beneath a flash tidal wave. The fourth, all Ontario's skyscrapers cracked and every church steeple in Quebec shattered. The fifth, sixth, seventh, eighth, ninth and tenth, brush fires laid waste to the wheat fields of the prairies, the Rocky Mountains tumbled into the foothills, the Arctic tundra was submerged beneath a vast inland sea, and in the southern cities, every shopping centre imploded, the subway tunnels caved in, and all the red-bricked walls in subdivisions were jolted into such odd angles one to the other, their houses would never resemble each other again.

As the plane rose, I looked through the window and saw the snow in Zurich was dissolving to water that flowed down the streets and into the lake as people ran outside clapping and dancing. With my face in my hands I wept loudly without restraint as cold winds thrashed my cheeks and snow poured down from a small cloud just below the carry-on luggage rack. Then over water I saw the Atlantic Ocean burst into flame and become one vast, boiling pit.

When I arrived in Toronto, I didn't know where I was. Everything had changed. The CN tower, which had been in the city centre, was in the north. Streets that ran east-west ran north-south or diagonally and vice versa. The city no longer had three islands in the lake but several. When I boarded the subway, I realized it'd been transformed into an amusement-park train that went in a circle around the business district while the old subway lines had been moved to the countryside so farmers could more easily transport cattle.

I tried to take a taxi home but forgot my street name and forgot my neighbourhood's name. I opened the book in a phone-booth to search for my number and corresponding address but the alphabet was in a new order beginning 'H R F' and ending 'B V E'.

Luckily I ran into the lady I play pin-the-tail with who pointed east (my apartment had been in the west) and said, 'One kilometre. Beside the oil refinery.' Toronto has an oil refinery? As I walked home, the ground kept fracturing beneath my feet. Lines would form in the pavement as I crossed the street. I had to jump over gulleys, steadily widening crevices, and when I reached the edge of a borough called South York and saw my apartment building in the distance, I had to cross a wind-filled ravine to reach it.

I entered my basement apartment and stood looking at my empty walls, my night-black computer screen.

Everything will be fine once I get back into my old routine, I thought. I can forget all that's happened and become my old complacent self again.

But when I looked at my rocks in their plastic boxes, I saw they'd changed from a bright red to pale grey like things that had died from want of oxygen.

And at night, my head on the pillow, I could hear it: the fire burning at the Earth's centre. Molten lava coagulates into steaming mounds that collapse into fragments that join other masses …

Days passed. Months passed. Years passed. And still I am wakened by Arctic winds pounding at my window. I see the bones of Franz's knuckles in stones that litter city construction sites, his kneecaps in the boulders that mark entrances to suburban parks, the ridge of his eyebrow in the curved rocks arching round the edges of bungalow flowerbeds, and when I try to shut him out and, by staring through a microscope lens, reduce the world to a circle a mere 0.20 microns in diameter, there in the lit rock are lines like the veins on the back of his leg and abrupt indentations that resemble the dimple in his chin.

I cannot escape. Though I have tried.

Six months after my return, I threw a stone across a river and started dating other men. I put an ad in the newspaper, 'Geologist seeks hot stud,' followed strangers onto newly built subway platforms, shook hands a second too long with terse-eyed men at house parties, and discreetly pressed my knee against the seam-strained, blue-jean-clad crotches of open-mouthed men on bar stools, who immediately ordered me drinks or put out their cigarettes and left.

I'd hoped sex would sear Franz from my mind and so made love in telephone booths, candlelit boudoirs, gas-station washrooms, stalled elevators, vinyl-cushioned bathtubs, on the top of the CN tower, but always my hand kept forgetting to cover my mouth that yawned uncontrollably, as my head continued to nod long after my partner had finished speaking.

I threw a stone across another river and started dating women. I mingled at office parties in companies I didn't work for, offered unmatched socks to brooding women in laundromats, mixed my letters with those in the mail-slots of single ladies in apartment-complexes, and my world became filled with the intoxicating odour of rose-petal perfume, the static crackle of fingernails running through long, red-dyed hair, the thick, humid, nylon-scented heat wafting from pantyhose left drying on the washroom radiator. But in bed I kept looking for body parts I'd thought had gotten lost in the covers but turned out not to have been there in the first place, and one day after giving a long affectionate speech I realized I was just mouthing the words to a pop song I'd heard on the radio that morning.

Then I threw a stone into a river and started dating hermaphrodites, transsexuals, men who were women and women who were men or both or neither or who didn't know. I dated people dressed as animals and animals dressed as people, and once spent an entire evening chatting with a panty-clad blow-up doll that I deflated and inflated for variety.

But amidst the myriad faces of the world's people who sat across the table from me in ten-star restaurants where vichyssoise and trout flambé were just the appetizers, where the tablecloth was piled high with long-stemmed roses, columbine blossoms and delphinium blooms whose dizzying perfume was stronger than the scent of tarragon, paprika and turmeric rising from our roasted duck, where Valentine's Day came twice a week, the violinist never left the table, and champagne bottles were popping non-stop, always as I finished my drink there was an ice cube bouncing against my lips, colliding with my teeth, chilling my tongue, skull, body, until, shivering, I had to run to the washroom where every solid object, the cubicle walls, gleaming chrome taps, the tin wastepaper basket, seemed a part of Franz's body.

If the world could stop spinning and I be released from its centrifugal forces to float ether-like into the outer atmosphere. But no. There is the ground forever beneath my feet, the fire burning at the Earth's centre, winds blowing one way, then another.

I wrote all Franz's good qualities (he laughs so readily, will never come to my home) in a scrapbook that I tried to burn, but the paper wouldn't catch. Then I tore out and flushed its pages down the toilet but the next day they returned, sentences flowing through my taps, swirling about the plates I eat off, shooting from the showerhead to saturate my body.

I have been surprised by midsummer snowstorms in the middle of supermarket parking lots, on department-store escalators, in dentists' waiting rooms, on lonely beaches where I pull rocks up from the earth.

I was not made for such drama. I was meant to live out my seventy-odd years in quiet obscurity and then be buried a mere two metres below the Earth's surface. I did not expect the world's subterranean plates to shift and collide. I did not expect the oceans of the world to conspire against me.

I gaze into horizons.

I shout into windstorms.

One night I finally raced into my backyard garden, flung myself onto the ground and clawed up fen rocks, morfite pebbles, veinstone, dolomite, burnstone, gypsum, travertine and rammed everything down my throat.

The next morning I woke up in Emergency.

Months later I spoke at a Toronto symposium.

I stood at the podium before people in rows that zigzagged as violently as the stitches on my stomach. The room was hot, and whirling fans rocked and buzzed. Fluorescent lights hummed and I could see the deepest wrinkles in everyone's faces.

'You think you are scientists,' I spoke very quietly, 'leading humanity to a better future. I am a scientist.' I said to myself, 'Do I have a future?' I lowered my head and then lifted it. 'You think air abrades sediment particles more efficiently than water? We've long thought this true but it's an oversimplification. On closer look it's a fallacy complete.'

People stared, foreheads lined.

Something inside me flashed. 'Few minerals are stable and rocks are only as stable as the environments that created them. Even subterranean lava flows are unstable for they crystallize at high temperatures. For the past two years I've been studying deposits on Alpine schistose.' My voice became husky. 'Their molecular structure has been constantly eroding and the quartz in various conglomerates could eventually degrade into bauxite. The extremity of the change shows that metamorphosis is simply inevitable in all organisms. Despite our research,' I lifted up a ream of unbound paper in my trembling hands, 'the current disequilibrium between rock, ice, air and water remains. Our analysis has unearthed nothing new.' The block of paper suddenly slipped from my fingers and disintegrated into hundred of individual sheets that got caught up in the jets of air from the rotating fans and spun in whirlwinds about the crowd like flocks of lost seagulls. I shouted, 'We should cease mining crystals that could have once offered theories concerning the movement of the Earth, and put away our seismometers and return these ridiculous rock samples to the forest beds we stole them from, or the stresses caused by all this activity will result in foliated slates, schists and gneisses and, as the ground we stand on is rock, if it fractures, what will become of us, ladies and gentlemen? What in God's name will become of us?'

My voice broke and I collapsed weeping on the podium. I pressed my face into the lacquered wood surface. Fan-blades stopped spinning. Data-crammed papers slid softly to the earth.

The world was silent.

Circles

Each Friday at Paul's we play games. Charades, slap-your-neighbour, crack-an-egg-on-your-cheek. Streetlights glow gold in the darkening outside and, giddy from Cheezies and root beer (Paul's in AA, insists 'no booze'), we become gloriously stupendously magnificently ridiculous. Henrietta balances on one leg, sings 'Oh Amsterdam.' Sam spins, blinking, chants 'I'm a lighthouse, a lighthouse.' I cry out, 'The Exorcist shall rid us of the demon of lethargy,' and laughter ricochets between bare walls. We fall back, the soft sofa moulding perfectly to our butts. In one corner the clock hangs and, if we remember not to look, it soon ceases to exist.

Then, one night, a new guest. Ron.

He has no lips, mouth or nose, only glaucous globulous eyes that attach to our every move, stick like leeches to the skin, cannot be shaken off.

Our motions decelerate. Voices fade.

In my Freshie-filled whisky glass, I see myself whole.

Ron says, 'Why do you all do this? I prefer to get to know people, have meaningful talks. For God's sakes, don't you see how foolish you all look.'

A bell has sounded and Henrietta, Sam, Paul and I gaze into each other's eyes, as half-visible clouds of whirling dust settle quietly on furniture.

Deflated, huddling together for warmth, we collapse onto the couch. In a new silence we soon decide that, okay, we will do it. We will talk. Very seriously. One to another.

We begin. First Paul, Nicole, myself, Sam. We share tales of childhood trauma: Paul's godmother washed his hair daily in cherry Jell-O; Nicole was once beaten with a stale baguette; parents constantly horked out our names like phlegm. And don't forget the horrifying present: our lovers, mouldy-breathed psychopaths who coat our genitals in Shake 'n' Bake and broadcast our flaws on the subway public address system; daily our workplace offices spin like crazed merry-go-rounds as colleagues vomit down mail slots, while shrieking neighbours pound on our apartment doors, landlords enclose bomb threats with rent increase notices, and cockroaches with tap-dance heels clatter through our dreams.

The air's heavy, and we sink to the floor to suck the dirt from carpet fronds.

Ron concludes, '... and afterwards my mother said I looked like Godzilla's excrement.'

We sigh. Is that finally everything?

I stare at the bare hanging bulb for a clue what to do next. A crack in the ceiling zigzags like a frenzied, seismic graph line.

Then an abrupt realization paints the walls neon topazine yellow: Everything in the world exhausts itself. Even tragedy can't go on forever.

The carpet changes to the speckled gold of rippling wheat, the light bulb is a silver, spinning disco-ball.

Sam shouts, 'Cock-a-doodle-do.' Pinball-machine lights start flashing as the couch slowly reinflates. Henrietta, then Nicole, Paul, Sam and I rise, each standing on one leg, arms flapping.

Acknowledgements

I thank Jack Illingworth for his insightful comments and guidance, Tim and Elke Inkster for their hard work, Tom Wayman for his indispensable advice, Dayle Berke for her ever-zealous reading of my writing. I am grateful to Brian Davis and Stephen Nunn for their openness and hospitality, Erica Bowen and Mary Frances Coady for their feedback, Jill Goldberg and Liane Keightley for their help. Also heartfelt thanks to Terrie Hamazaki, John Mingolla, Steve Slessor, Jean-Pierre Bonhomme and Jean-François Roulier for their encouragement and support.

I thank everyone involved in the Banff Centre May Writing Studio 2003, especially Mark Jarman and Zsuzsi Gartner.

Acknowledgement is made of the following publications, in which versions of some stories in the collection appeared: *Event, Fiddlehead, Prairie Fire, Matrix, Dalhousie Review, lichen, Quickies 3, Short Stuff* and *Other Voices*. Special thanks to Rob Allen for submitting 'Enough' (published as 'Sucking Price-Tags') for the Journey Prize, Andris Taskans for nominating 'The Whereabouts of Lost Melodies' (published as 'Barriers') for the Western Magazine Award and Cathy Stonehouse for nominating 'The Royal Conservatory' for a National Magazine Award.

I am grateful for generous support from the Canada Council for the Arts and the Toronto Arts Council.

Barry Webster is a classically trained pianist and a graduate of the University of Toronto and Concordia University. His fiction has appeared in numerous Canadian journals from the *Fiddlehead* to the *Danforth Review* and has been short-listed for a National Magazine Award and the CBC-Quebec Prize. Originally from Toronto, he lives in East Montreal.